YANKEE BOY

Rickie Wood-Bovée

Rickie Wood-Bovee

With

Jim Bovay

Rickie Wood-Bovee with Jim Bovay

© 2013 Rickie Wood-Bovee & Jim Bovay

All rights reserved.

Published by Three Bars Publishing

Ponce de Leon, FL

Visit our website at www.threebarspublishing.com

Printed in the United States

ISBN: 978-0-9912546-2-0

Library of Congress Control Number: 2014935336

On the cover: Hunter Chilcutt as the 'Yankee Boy'

Yankee Boy

We would like to dedicate this book to Jodi Brooks, our mail carrier and one of our most ardent supporters. When we told her about the idea for this book she kept at us until we wrote it, so thank you, Jodi for keeping us focused on this story. I think you'll like it.

All names and places in this book are fictional, although Ponce de Leon and DeFuniak Springs are real towns in Florida. Any resemblance of characters to persons, living or dead is purely coincidental. All incidences are fictional and a work of the author's imagination. The one exception is the Asboth raid on Marianna in 1864. That was a real action during the Civil War. Pensacola was a hotspot during our nation's fractional war. The Union had an active base at Pensacola and Fort Barrancas remained in Union Hands, although surrounded by Confederate Forces.

Rickie Wood-Bovee with Jim Bovay

Author's Note

The idea for this story first started germinating when I read an article in our local newspaper about the discovery of some very old grave markers in the Ponce de Leon community.

This community lies just east of my favorite subject location, DeFuniak Springs. Both are located in the Florida panhandle. This area is ripe in Victorian and pre-Victorian history and culture and we, my husband Jim and I, live right in the midst of these two communities.

If you've read our biographical information you know that we traveled the country in our pre-retirement days so our description of the drive the kids took, especially into New Jersey, New York and New England were made from our memory of those areas.

We hope that you enjoy this story as much as we enjoyed writing it.

Acknowledgements

We would like to thank Dan Owens for his untiring support and advice. He is always there when needed.

We would like to thank Jodi Brooks for her support. She is always there with enthusiasm.

We would also like to thank those who, every year, reenact those decisive events when our country nearly broke in two. Those from both sides fought for what they believed and today there are those who like to keep their memory alive perhaps to make sure that we, as a country, don't let the same thing happen again.

We would also like to thank Bruce Naylor, a local Real Estate Agent, who first inspired this story by reporting his discovery of the ancient grave markers.

It is also important that we thank the principal of Ponce de Leon High School, Mr. Brown, for his help. He advised us as to the disciplinary procedures at the school.

A big thank you to Hunter Chilcutt for being our 'Yankee Boy'. He and his family are Frontier Reenactors and Hunter slipped into this role quite comfortably.

Rickie Wood-Bovee with Jim Bovay

Chapter One
1861

The raging winds swept the waves into a frothy wild morass as it tried to beat the ship into submission. As he made his way across the deck, the young lad was caught up in the raging waters of the Gulf of Mexico and was swept overboard.

No one knew he was gone and even if they did there was nothing they could do. The young lad was on his own and he knew his survival depended on his ability to make it to shore before the wind and the waves overcame him. He struggled against the raging weather barely able to keep his head above the surface, but somehow he knew he would make it. He prayed to God to let him live; to let him gain the land and not die a nameless victim of the tides.

Some time later, and he couldn't have told you how long for it seemed like hours and surely was, his feet touched bottom. The waves were still moving him along as they raged against the land, but now he could see land, and at last, he could feel it beneath his feet. He used his arms, which now felt like lead weights, and he used his legs to propel himself toward the beach. No one was there to help, not in this weather. The beaches were bare, but he struggled until he was able to drag himself on hands and knees up upon the sand and beyond the reach of the waves.

He finally collapsed; his head lay heavily against his arms and his body into the sand. When he awoke, the screaming winds had stopped and the air was nearly silent. Just the soft sounds of gentle waves caressing the sands filled his ears. He closed his eyes and drifted off again with the knowledge he was safe from Neptune's vengeance.

He awoke again to the sound of voices and as he raised his head he saw the forms of soldiers in blue rushing toward him. He smiled and dropped his head onto his arms once more.

Chapter Two

2012

Sara stared out the car window as it moved swiftly along the highway. She wasn't looking at anything in particular, just staring as the scenery whizzed past her line of sight.

Sara was angry; angry at her parents, angry at the circumstances, angry at the world. As the scenery sped by, Sara thought about what had brought her here, speeding toward Florida and a place she knew nothing about.

She really couldn't blame her father; this was his moment. He was an aspiring writer and just a few months back he had finally hit it big. He had sold a manuscript he had been working on for several years to a big publisher with an option for a second novel.

The paycheck had been sizable and Sara's parents had been able to pay off all their bills, but now… now the whole family was heading for Ponce de Leon, Florida.

Sara thought back to the night her parents had told her about the move; "Ponce de what" she had asked.

"Sara, it's so your dad can concentrate on his writing. It's a small town in the Florida panhandle; Ponce de Leon; you know, like the explorer," Sara's mom had explained.

"Yeah, but Mom, why now? I'm just going to start high school; all my friends are here and…" Sara began to cry as she threw herself down on her bed and buried her face in her pillow.

Sara's father joined in, "Look, kitten, I know this is sudden, but this is a great opportunity for me. We've got enough money I won't have to work and neither will your mom, unless she wants to.

Sara lifted her head from the pillow, "But Daddy, why do we have to move? Why now?"

"Look honey, this move is a financial decision. The house in Florida was left to me by your grandma and it's been sitting vacant for over a year. Its rent free; we don't owe any money on it and all we'll have to pay is utilities. Here, where we live now, the rent is over fifteen hundred a month."

"Mom, please, can't it wait. I won't know anybody in Ponsa whatzits name. I'll be miserable; I'll hate it, I just know I will."

"I'm sorry, Sara, but this is just the way it has to be. Maybe in a year or two we can take a trip back here to see everyone."

Sara's eyes bugged out and her expression was one of fright, "A year or two? Mom, everyone will have forgotten me. I won't know anybody here by then either. Ooohhh!" Sara flung her face back down into her pillow to bury her sorrow.

As the car hurdled toward Florida, Sara's little brother was another story. Whereas, Sara was fourteen, soon to be fifteen, and suffering angst over the move, her younger brother, Eddie was ten and his excitement at the move was overflowing. He looked out one side of the car windows and then would move over to Sara's side and look out her windows. As he squeezed over her to get a view out of Sara's side, Eddie accidentally pinched Sara with her seat belt.

"Mo'om," Sara had a way of making extra syllables where none should be when she was aggravated with her brother.

"Eddie, sit back down and leave Sara alone."

"Ah, geez, Mom, there was a neat looking horse on her side. All I got on my side is nothing." Eddie sat down with a decided plop as he looked out his own window.

They were now traveling south of Dothan, Alabama and definitely in farming country. The narrow, two lane highway was bordered on each side by mile after mile of fields; some white with cotton, some with lush green plants they would later learn were okra and soybeans and especially peanuts.

In between the fields were rows of lush green trees, some pines, but many that would lose their lushness when the winter temperatures set in.

The one thing that Sara did not see was stores; shopping malls, strip malls, or even an occasional Wal-Mart. As she looked around, those had all disappeared miles back. Her thoughts ran to the solitude and remoteness, *I might as well be in a desert. I haven't seen a living thing except that one crummy horse, oh, wait... there's a cow, whoopee!*

"Mom, are we going to live near a town? Please say yes."

"Sara, I don't know. I don't know any more than you do. Ask your father, he's been here before."

Sara turned her gaze toward her father, "Dad, please tell me that there is at least some civilization where we are going."

"Well, gee, honey, it's been a long time since I've been here; probably thirty, maybe thirty-five years. I just remember being out in the country. You know, farms and cows, and horses; stuff like that."

Sara moaned loudly and buried her head in her hand and leaned against the window once again. Before long she had fallen asleep.

Within fifteen minutes they passed a road sign that stated 'Leaving Alabama' and then soon after another that stated 'Welcome to Sunny Florida'.

Sara was jolted out of her sleep when Eddie yelled, "Yippee, we're almost there."

Sara looked around disoriented for just a moment and then realized that they were still moving rapidly along the country highway. "Mom can you make him be quiet. I was asleep and he woke me up." Sara leaned her head back against the window and her misery oozed out of every pore.

After about fifteen minutes she sat up, looking out at the passing fields as the car slowed, "Well, folks, I think we have arrived." Sara's dad announced.

The car turned into a long lane and moved toward an older looking two story house. They drove toward the house and to Sara it looked like something out of 'Little House on the Prairie' without the sod roof. The house was surrounded by fields of grass and off to the back were thick lush woods. No other houses in sight.

The car pulled up to the side of the house and her dad turned off the motor. The engine had not even ceased to idle and Eddie was bounding out his door, "Come on, Sara, let's check the place out."

Sara just sighed, hard and heavy, imagining that Eddie would be her sole companion until school started. She leaned forward and pleaded with her mother, "Mo'om, do I have to?'

"Sara, humor your brother; what else have you got to do. Dad and I will get the luggage and meet you in the house." By the time Sara made it into the house, Eddie had already run through the lower floor, checking out the rooms, and was now clattering up the stairs to the second floor.

Sara stepped in through the front door and was stopped in her tracks by the smell of mold and decay. She turned around and stepped back out onto the front porch with a disgusted expression on her face.

Her mother walked up, and noticing Sara's expression asked, "For heaven's sake, what is the matter?"

"Mom, it stinks. I can't go in there."

"Well, of course it stinks. The house hasn't been opened in almost a year. This is a hot and moist climate; things mildew."

Jean, Sara's mother, stepped in through the door and exclaimed, "Whew, I guess it stinks. Sara, come help me open some windows so we can air the place out."

Sara sighed heavily, took a deep breath and stepped quickly into the room and toward the closest window. She flicked the window latch and lifted the old wooden window up and pushed her head forward as if to inhale a huge gulp of fresh outdoor air, and rammed her face into the screen.

Hitting the screen made her gasp, losing the air she had inhaled outside. To again fill her lungs she inhaled through the screen, taking in a large quantity of dust that had collected there. This sent Sara into a coughing fit and made her eyes water. She was miserable. She hated what her life had come to.

Eddie called from the top of the stairs, "Sara! Hey, Sara, come up here so we can decide who gets what bedroom. I want to get unpacked.

At that moment Jack, Sara's father bumped through the front door, hauling several suitcases at once, "Whew, this place stinks! "

"Exactly, Dad. That's what I've been saying; do we have to stay here tonight? Can't we go find a motel?" Sara was beginning to whine, she was so miserable.

"Sara, quit whining. We have spent our allotted money on motels already. We'll just tough it here until we can get things cleaned up. Here, get your suitcase and take it up to your room." Sara did not question her dad; she just picked up her suitcase and clomped up the stairs.

When she got to the second floor, the heat was stifling, "Oh my God, it's like an oven up here! Mom, doesn't this place have air conditioning?"

Jean had come upstairs ahead of Sara and was staking out their bedroom and a den for Jack so that the kids could choose their rooms. Thankfully, this was a fairly large house with enough rooms to meet all their needs.

Jean walked into the room that Sara had claimed for her own, "Sara, will you quit complaining. This is a big adjustment for all of us and it's going to take time for us to get all the kinks ironed out, so, please, honey, be patient and quit complaining."

Sara looked at her mother, pushed out her lower lip, and stated, "Nobody understands what I'm going through. This whole move is a disaster for me and I am not happy."

"Sara, I know this is hard… honey, I've left behind friends, too, but I'm willing to make the sacrifice for your father; aren't you?"

Now Sara felt very small; ashamed of her pouty attitude, "I'm sorry, Mom. This is just so new. I'm a city girl, not some country bumpkin. What am I gonna do for friends or a social life... I don't even know how to square dance."

Sara was nearing tears again when her mother interrupted, "Sara, why don't you go explore outside. Those woods looked interesting, and you've always liked to hike."

Sara looked at her mother, her eyes showing total surprise, "Mom, I've always hiked in parks with nicely groomed trails and signs to tell you where you were going. I've never just gone 'out in the woods'; I might get lost."

Jean smiled lightly, "Then don't go in very deep, and just remember, if you get disoriented, sit down where you are and just start calling. We'll hear you."

Sara sighed and figured *what have I got to lose?* So she changed her tennis shoes to her hiking boots and headed down the stairs.

On the first floor, heading out the door, she came across her dad, struggling through the front door with three more suitcases, trying to fit all three, plus his legs, through the doorway at the same time, and was now stuck. He heard her coming down the stairs and looked up, his eyes telling her he needed help. Sara grabbed one of the suitcases and pulled it free of the jam, allowing her father to break free.

Once the doorway was cleared, Sara headed out the door. "Where ya goin' Kitten?" her father called after her.

"I'm taking a walk to check out the woods."

"Watch for snakes." Her father hollered out to her.

Sara stopped dead in her tracks, turned, and looked at her dad, her eyes practically popping out of their sockets, "Snakes?"

Her dad was bouncing his head in a bobble doll kind of way, "Yeah, there's snakes down here."

"What kind of snakes?"

"Well, some friendly and some not so friendly."

"Have you told mom?"

"No, but let me tell her the good news. You know how she feels about snakes. Just keep your eyes on the ground and walk slow enough, if you see one, you can take an alternate route."

Sara smiled a half-hearted smile at her dad and muttered to herself, "*Great, just great!*"

She headed out across the porch and down the steps; moving around to the back of the house and toward the line of woods that seemed to circle the grassy fields in a wide arc. She headed directly back from the house passing a couple of out buildings on her way. She looked at each of the structures wondering what they might have been. One looked like it might have been a chicken coop, the second just some sort of storage shed; she noticed a couple of tools hanging inside.

Sara was careful not to go inside either building because of the possibilities of snakes, and because of the huge spider webs that seemed to be growing all over the buildings, inside and out.

Sara slowly made her way to the edge of the woods and peered in through some heavy brush. She walked along the edge of the foliage, watching the ground for snakes, but stopping now and then to look inside the tree line. She came across a couple of old creek beds and catalogued them for later exploration. After wandering along for what seemed like only a few minutes, she looked back at the house and realized she had come almost to the end of the tree line and the grassy field. The house was just a small bump on the horizon.

Sara looked across the expanse of grass and imagined how many snakes might be lurking there and then she looked toward the road, which was just a few yards from where she stood. Sara decided that traversing the few yards to the road and then walking the pavement back to the house made much more sense that trying to dodge snakes in the field.

It took her only a few minutes to make it to the road and walking back to the house was a breeze from there. As she walked along, she heard the sound of a vehicle coming toward her. As it neared, she noticed it was an older model pickup truck. The truck slowed as it rumbled past her and then stopped just beyond where she stood. Turning around, she looked at the young man, the sole occupant of the truck, who climbed out from the driver's side. He had on an old straw cowboy hat, the brim nearly rolled up, and as he approached he took the hat off and held it in his hands in front of his huge western style belt buckle.

He walked up to where Sara stood, bowing his head slightly, his light brown hair falling over his forehead, and then in that soft southern drawl so prevalent here, he said, "Thought I'd stop and say howdy; you the new folks livin' in the Elkins house? Didn't recnize ya so I thought ya might be. I'm yor neighbor; live jus' up the road. Names Tyler... Tyler Infinger." The young man nodded his head again and gave Sara a soft and friendly smile.

Sara smiled back and then introduced herself, "Hi, I'm Sara Richardson, and yes, we just arrived today. I was just exploring the woods a little bit."

Tyler nodded his head again, "Best watch for snakes this time a year."

"So I've been told."

"Well, gotta go. Headin' to Wal-Mart to git some stuff for my mom."

"You mean there's a Wal-Mart? What about other stores, a mall, maybe?" Sara looked at Tyler with a hopeful expression.

Tyler shook his head from side to side, "Nah, closest mall is Dothan, maybe Panama City. And then there's Fort Walton

Beach."

Sara's face fell, "Oh."

"But, hey, aroun' here, Wal-Mart's the happenin' place. All the kids meet in the parkin' lot on Friday and Saturday nights; so it's not so bad. Some night, once I've met yor folks, I'll take you with me."

"I'd like that," Sara smiled at Tyler.

"Well, gotta go. See ya later." Tyler smiled and snugged his hat onto his head, rocking it back and forth slightly, and returned to his truck. Sara watched as the truck clattered out of sight.

Sara resumed her walk to her new home with just a little more spring in her step.

Chapter Three

Sara entered the house to a mass of confusion. The moving truck had arrived and the driver, a helper, her dad and mom were all moving boxes and furniture in a rush to get everything into the house. There were boxes everywhere.

Sara stood in the doorway momentarily until one of the moving guys came up behind her and made a noise like he was clearing his throat, "Excuse me, miss, I need to get through."

Sara turned to see the guy holding another box and looked like he was ready to put it down, anywhere. Sara's mom walked into the front room from the kitchen and when she saw Sara, exclaimed, "Oh, Sara, boy, am I glad you're back. Grab a box marked kitchen and help me in here, will you, babe?"

Sara looked through the assorted boxes until she spotted one marked 'kitchen' as her mom disappeared into the other room.

Sara walked into the kitchen carrying a box that felt like it contained the kitchen sink, "Geez, Mom, what's in these boxes?"

"Hard telling, Sweetie, could be almost anything.

Towards the end there, I was just putting anything and everything in a box just to get done. We'll just have to open it and see."

Sara cut open the tape sealing the box and found a can of coffee in with the coffee maker, mixer, and electric fry pan. "Well, at least you can have your morning coffee and cook us dinner." Sara smiled at her mother.

"That walk must have improved your mood, or so it seems."

"Mom, I followed the tree line until I was close to the road and then walked back by way of the road. I met a guy; he's our neighbor and his name is Tyler."

Jean chuckled, "That explains the change in attitude," and she nodded her head a couple of times.

Sara looked a little chastened and lowered her head slightly as she smiled.

"How old is Tyler?" Jean asked her daughter.

"I don't know; the subject of age didn't come up, but I'm assuming he's at least sixteen cuz he was driving a pickup; going to the Wal-Mart for his mom."

Jean just nodded her head slightly and smiled a knowing smile, "See, I told you it wouldn't take long for you to make friends. Your Dad says the people are really friendly around here."

Sara started to go out to the front room to get another box when her mother called after her, "Sara, did Tyler say how far the Wal-Mart was?"

Sara shook her head 'no' as her Dad walked through the doorway, "Tyler who; who's Tyler?" Sara disappeared into the other room as her dad did a three-sixty turn trying to get an answer to his question.

"A neighbor boy Sara just met on the road. I think his last name is Infinger."

"Really? Well, the Infingers have lived around here for years. They were the next house up the road when I came to visit my grandparents years ago; nice family."

"Apparently he made a favorable impression on Sara because she came back in a much better mood."

"Well, I'll have to thank Tyler when we meet him."

By early evening the movers were gone and although the front room looked like a warehouse depository, things were slowly disappearing from the chaotic mess into the other rooms.

Most of the furniture had been taken directly to their appointed rooms, so Sara spent the rest of the evening rearranging her bedroom and hanging her mementos on the walls. By bed time she had her room pretty well set up and when finished she called her mom in to give her approval.

Jean stopped at the door, scanning the room and all of its accoutrements, "Oh, Sara, it looks really nice; you have been busy."

Sara smiled at her mother's approval. I love my window, too, Mom. It looks out onto some of the woods. It's a really nice view."

Jean walked over to the window. Looking out she could see what Sara was talking about, "There's only one problem, honey. This is a southern exposure and I'm very positive that we may have to put you in some sort of auxiliary air conditioning in here. With the intense heat here in the summer, the sun is going to beat down on your room with a vengeance."

"Can we just put heavy curtains up, Mom, to block the sun?"

"Yes, we could do that, but you'll lose your view, plus the walls will just heat things up anyway. We'll just see about a window air for you besides the central air conditioning that we have. It'll be a lot cooler for you to sleep."

"Whatever you say, Mom; I'm not going to complain.

A couple of days later when the heavy unpacking was finished, Sara was up in her room when she heard a familiar sounding vehicle rumble to a stop just outside their house.

Sara went running down the stairs stopping just short of the front door... until she heard a knock on the door.

She opened the door to find Tyler standing there holding

his hat as before, and as she saw him and smiled, he nodded his head and returned her smile, "Hello Tyler, nice to see you again."

"Howdy, Sara. I just dropped by to say hello and meet yor parents. Friday's comin up and remember what I told you about Fridays and Saturdays. Thought you might like to come along, so thought I'd better git over here and meet yor folks."

Sara smiled even wider, "Won't you come in. I'll call my Mom and Dad." Sara walked a few steps over to the staircase, "Dad, can you come down here for a minute."

A distant voice answered, "Be right there, Kitten."

Sara turned to Tyler, an embarrassed smile on her face, "That's his nickname for me; he's called me that as long as I can remember." Then Sara went to the kitchen door, "Mom, could you come in here for a minute; Tyler's here to meet you."

Jean soon appeared at the doorway, and a huge smile spread across her face as she approached the two teens. Sara's dad was making his way down the stairs at almost the same time. When they were both gathered at the front, Jean asked Tyler, "Would you like to sit down?" and she motioned toward the couch.

Tyler moved over and sat, saying as he moved, "Thank you, ma'am. I cain't really stay too long. I just wanted to come and introduce myself. I met Sara the other day and, well, the kids around here don't have a whole lot to do, especially during the summer. And, well, we gather at the local Wal-Mart parking lot on Fridays and Saturdays, just to git t'gether and talk, ya know, that sort of stuff. And, well, I told Sara she could come with me if'n you folks didn't mind, but I wanted ta meet you folks so's ya'll would know who Sara was with."

Sara looked pleadingly at her parents, but did not say anything.

Jean looked at Jack and then back at Tyler, "That's very nice of you, Tyler. Do you mind if I ask you a few questions?"

"No, ma'am, I don't."

"Well, how old are you, Tyler?"

"Sixteen, ma'am; I'll be in the eleventh grade. Go to Ponce de Leon High School."

"Oh, that just about answers my questions. What time do you usually come home?"

"Well, some of 'em stay out there until eleven or twelve, but I don't usually stay that late. My folks gave me a curfew and I have to be home by ten thirty, So's I usually leave aroun' ten. But if'n you give me a time when Sara has to be home, I'll have her here."

"Well, if you don't mind that we don't give you an answer right this instant, I guarantee you that we will give it serious consideration. If you could just call Sara back, say, by Thursday, she can give you the answer then. Would that be alright with you?"

"Yes, ma'am; it shorely would." Tyler stood and made a turn toward the door, "Well, I gotta go now; it was plum nice to meet you folks." Tyler nodded his head toward the couple and then he turned his attentions toward Sara, "I'll call you Thursday." Tyler moved to the door and said goodbye to Sara and then left the house.

Sara had just closed the door when another knock was heard. She opened the door to Tyler standing there, hat in hand and an embarrassed expression, "I fergot to git yor phone number."

After Tyler left, Sara retreated to her room to let her Mom and Dad discuss the situation. She had learned long ago not to press an issue with her parents. They would discuss it fairly and usually came up with an agreeable decision... except for the move down here. But now, things weren't looking too bad.

Chapter Four

Wednesday rolled around and Sara went to her Mom, "Am I going to be able to go with Tyler Friday night?"

Dad and I discussed it. We like Tyler; he seems like a really nice young man. And I think you need to get to know some of the local kids before school starts, so…"

Sara was anxiously awaiting her mother's response. Expecting the worst, but hoping for the best.

"Yes, with one condition, we want you home by ten."

Sara started to object and just opened her mouth to do so, when her mother continued, "Take it or leave it, kiddo. This is the first time out; we don't know the other kids and you will be a ways away so, at least for this time, be home by ten.

Sara stood there staring at her mother considering everything and decided it wasn't worth arguing about; at least she would get to go. Sara smiled at her mother, "Thanks, Mom."

Sara left quickly for her room and once upstairs, as she passed the door to her father's den, she leaned her head through the door, and said, "Thanks, Dad."

Jack turned from his computer just in time to see Sara's head disappear behind the door jam, "You're welcome, I guess" he answered, confused about what he had been thanked for, shrugged his shoulders and then went back to his writing.

Sara went into her room to look through her clothes to try and decide what to wear Friday. Eddie poked his head in her door, "Sara, wanna go out and explore a little bit, maybe hike through the woods with me?"

"Not now, Eddie, I'm busy."

"Doin' what; don't look like you're busy to me."

Sara turned from her closet to face Eddie, "I'm busy looking at my clothes; do you mind?"

"I don't mind, but what are you looking at your clothes for. They haven't changed since we got here."

"Eddie, go away, will you?"

"Aw geez, you're no fun. Come on, it won't hurt you to go outside for a little bit."

"Go away or I'm gonna call Mom."

"Geez." Eddie disappeared out the door.

Friday evening arrived and Sara was too nervous to eat when Jean called everyone to dinner. Tyler was due to pick her up in less than an hour and she had too much to do, "Mom, I still have to shower and get my hair ready. Besides, I'm not hungry."

"Sara, it's going to be a long time until you get home."

"Mom, I'll take a couple of dollars with me and if I get hungry I can walk into Wal-Mart and buy some chips."

"Sara, chips do not constitute a meal. Will you at least have some salad before you leave?"

Sara sighed, "Okay, but let me get my shower first, then after I fix my hair, I'll come down and eat some salad."

Tyler was right on time. He rolled to a stop next to their house at seven o'clock. Not to appear over anxious, Sara waited until he knocked on the door before she opened it. She was just finishing a mouthful of salad and swallowed it down quickly as she opened the door, "Hi, Tyler, please come in."

Tyler acknowledged Sara's parents, "Howdy, Mr. and Mrs. Richardson." Tyler had already removed his hat and now he nodded his head towards the two adults.

As Sara stepped forward, ready to leave, Tyler remarked to Jean and Jack, "I'll have Sara home by ten, don't chu worry."

Jean smiled, "Thank you, Tyler."

The ride into DeFuniak Springs, where the Wal-Mart was located, took about fifteen minutes and the two teens made small talk as they drove west on Hwy 90 to their destination.

When they finally pulled into the parking lot, Sara looked to where at least ten pick-up trucks were already gathered. They were all parked off into one corner of the parking lot and had parked in a circle so that the beds of the trucks were all facing in pin wheel fashion. The backs of the trucks were full of smiling, rollicking teens.

Once Tyler parked his truck, which completed the pin wheel, he got out, leaving the radio on and playing at high volume, and Sara followed him to the back where they climbed into the truck bed to sit on the sides. Soon other teens were walking over to greet Tyler and to meet Sara.

Before long Tyler was involved in conversations with some of the guys and several of the girls had come over to talk with Sara, greeting her as if she was an old friend.

Somewhere along the way, someone had slipped a beer into Sara's hand. She looked at the can of beer and thought, *if I take even one drink of this my folks will know and I'll never be able to set foot out of the house again.* Sara smiled weakly at the giver and quietly thanked them.

Sara sat on the hard edge of the truck for some time listening to the conversations going on around her. Everything being said was about hunting, their hunting dogs, and even their pick-up trucks. Sara was no Einstein, but even she could talk about music or books, or something other than hunting, dogs and pick-up trucks.

Well after dark, Sara knew it had to be time to head for home, so she stepped over to Tyler, "Tyler, it must be time for me to head for home."

"Oh, yeah, sure; we'll go right now."

Sara did not know how many beers Tyler, or anyone else might have had, but she hoped that he was sober enough to drive, but what happened next made her concern a moot point.

They said their goodbyes, and Tyler got behind the wheel. He turned the key, and nothing happened. All Sara heard was a small clicking sound coming from under the hood.

Tyler slammed his palms against the steering wheel and hollered out, "Dag nabbit!"

"What's wrong?" Sara asked.

"Battry's dead; dag nabbit!"

Tyler stuck his head out the window and called back to the group, "Anybody got some jumper cables?"

Sara looked back over the seat and out the rear window as one head after another swiveled back and forth in denial.

"Dag nabbit; dag nabbit, dag nabbit!" Sara could tell that Tyler was frustrated. He climbed out of the truck and went back to confer with some of his buddies and when he returned he told Sara, "It's five minutes to ten. Jim Bob said he'll take you home if you want."

"Oh, gosh, if I come home with someone else, Mom and Dad will never let me out until I'm twenty."

"Okay then, here's what we're gonna do," Tyler explained the next action to get his truck started. He waved out his window and the next thing Sara knew the truck was slowly rolling forward, now being pushed by every guy in attendance; Tyler motioned her behind the wheel as he opened his door and started pushing as well which left Sara to steer. This was a totally new experience for her.

As soon as they got the truck free of the pin wheel formation, Tyler got in behind the wheel as another truck pulled up behind and slowly rolled into the back of Tyler's pick-up until it bumped and they started to roll at a faster pace.

Tyler steered the truck out the parking lot driveway, down a slight slope, and when he came to Bob Sikes road, steered a hard left turn until the truck was moving slowly away from Wal-Mart on that road.

The push truck then closed the gap once again and when contact was made, the driver accelerated until Sara could see the speedometer bouncing toward twenty.

Tyler looked at Sara, "Don't worry, I've done this before. Once I get up nuff speed, I'll jus pop the clutch and this old girl will jus perk right up, and away toward home we'll be headin'."

Sara did not say anything; she just smiled a small, but doubtful smile.

The truck speedometer was now nearing twenty five when Tyler said, "Okay, here goes." He pushed in on the clutch, shifted the lever into first gear and then suddenly released the pressure on the clutch. The truck lurched forward a couple of hard times and then Sara heard a horrifying sound of metal hitting something hard.

She looked over at Tyler and saw his eyes open wider than she had ever seen them before and then, with his knuckles white from holding the steering wheel so tight, he yelled, "Oh, c**p!" He let out a huge sigh and as his truck slowed to a stop, Tyler's head fell to the steering wheel where it stayed. He mumbled a few words that Sara couldn't make out, which was probably for the better.

"Tyler, what's happened; why have we stopped?"

Tyler threw his head back and it slammed against the back window. When his head made contact the brim of his hat hit the rear window forcing the front of the hat right off his head leaving it hovering at a forty-five degree angle above his forehead. "I'm dead. Your folks are gonna kill me an my dad is gonna kill me and my truck is now dead."

Tyler got out of the truck and Sara turned in the seat looking out the back window. Tyler had walked about thirty feet behind the truck and was now looking down at a mass of metal littering the roadway. Some of his buddies were gathering around and as they patted Tyler on the back she could hear some of the comments, "Tough luck, Buddy"..."Man, what a mess."

Sara did not exactly know what had happened, but she was smart enough to realize, it was definitely after ten, and her folks would be steaming, *I have got to get home*, she thought to herself. She climbed out of the truck and walked back to where Tyler was mourning the loss of whatever was lying in the road. "Does anyone have a cell phone?"

"Jenny does," somebody answered. Sara looked around to find who had spoken. A tall blond guy named Charlie stepped forward and said, "She's back at the parking lot. I'll drive you back. Need to call yor folks?"

Sara nodded her head slowly as she muttered, "They're gonna kill me as it is; I was supposed to be home by ten." Charlie looked at his watch, "Oops, it's quarter til 'leven." Charlie's truck had been the push truck and now they climbed in to ride back to the Wal-Mart.

Sara turned to the window, "That's not what I needed to hear right now, but thanks anyway, Charlie."

Sara's folks understood when she explained the situation, but what they did not understand was why it had taken her so long to call, "Sara, we have been sitting here for nearly an hour. Why didn't you call when Tyler first had trouble getting his truck started?

"I don't know, Mom. I just didn't think about it."

"Well, we'll discuss this at a later time. Do we need to come and get you?"

"No, I don't think so; let me ask," Sara said quietly. Sara turned toward Charlie, "I hate to ask you, Charlie, but can you take me home; I live right out by Tyler."

"Shor, no problem."

Sara turned back to the phone, "Mom, there's a guy here who said he'll bring me home."

"Do you think he's trustworthy?"

"Of course, Mother. I'm not stupid. All these kids are nice." Sara did not mention the beer.

Jean hesitated for a moment, "Okay, then, just get home as soon as you can."

"Okay." Sara had been getting more and more depressed as one disaster after another had presented itself, but now that her mom knew what was going on she felt better about the situation. Now all she had to do was get home.

Chapter Five

Charlie pulled his truck into the drive and stopped his truck next to Sara's house. Sara noticed as they approached the house that only one light was on and that was the light in her mom and dad's room.

"You want me to walk you to the door?"

"No, thank you, Charlie; I can make it okay." Sara stepped out of the truck and then turned back to Charlie, "Thank you, again, for bringing me home. It was very nice of you, Charlie."

"No problem, Sara. I was glad to do it. Now I gotta go back and help Tyler git his truck home. See ya later, Sara."

Sara stepped away from the truck, slammed the door, and headed for her house. She opened the front door and was met by silence; everything was quiet in the house. With all of the lights out, Sara moved slowly toward the staircase and once she knew she was at the steps, she climbed slowly and quietly toward her bedroom.

When she reached the top of the stairs, she turned and headed toward her room. She saw the light coming from under the door to her parent's room and tip toed past. Just as she reached her door, her mother's voice came through the door, "Sara, we are going to talk in the morning."

"Okay, Mom."

Sara entered her room knowing that in the morning, she was going to have to defend her actions. As Sara lay in bed she tried to rehearse what she was going to say, knowing all too well that it would be worthless; how could she defend what happened this evening?

The next morning as Sara made her way down to breakfast, she passed her dad on the stairs, "Good morning, Kitten."

"Good morning, Dad." Sara tried to identify any bad omens in her father's attitude, but it did not work. Her dad seemed the same as always.

Sara entered the kitchen just as Eddie took his last bite of food. He looked up at her and said, "Mom. I'm goin' outside until the storm is over." Eddie stood quickly and made for the back door letting the screen slam behind him. The loud bang jarred both Sara and her mother.

"Good morning, Mom."

"Good morning, Sara."

Oh, oh, Sara thought. The negative vibes were definitely coming through from her mom.

"Mom…" Sara started

Jean held up a hand to indicate 'not a word'.

"But…" Sara tried again.

"Sara, I am very disappointed in your behavior last night."

"But Mom, it wasn't my fault. Tyler's truck wouldn't start when it was time to leave and nobody had any jumper cables, whatever those are. So they tried to push it to get the truck started and then something happened, I don't know what, but it left metal parts all over the road."

"Sara, I'm not concerned about Tyler's truck, I'm sorry he had trouble…"

"But, Mom, that's why I was late."

"I understand that, Sara. What your Dad and I are angry about is that you waited so long to call us. Why didn't you call us as soon as Tyler's truck wouldn't start?"

"Because I didn't think to."

"Exactly! Sara, your father and I sat here for almost an hour not knowing what might have happened. I was getting very concerned and frankly quite frightened."

"But, Mom, I was fine."

"Sara, we didn't know that."

Sara hung her head in shame, knowing she should have called somehow.

"When you start dating, which I do not consider last night a date, there is a certain amount of responsibility that goes along with the privilege; that is a responsibility to be home when you should and when you can't make it, you call and let us know what is going on... Okay, so here's the deal. It's now the middle of July and school around here starts the middle of August. Until school starts, no more outings unless we are there..."

"But Mom..."

"Sara, no buts; this is the way it's going to be. No argument."

"But Mom, there's nothing to do around here."

"Look, Sara, we are going to get a satellite receiver and then we can get satellite TV and Internet. And I am going to talk further with your Dad about getting one of those pay-as-you-go phones."

Sara's eyes lit up.

"It will be shared by everyone in the household. Whenever I go to the store or your Dad has to go somewhere, that phone will go with that person as an emergency contingency. It will not be for socializing and will not be for any other use but emergencies. Got it?"

Sara nodded her head in compliance. "Can I go now?"

"You haven't eaten anything."

"I'm not hungry, besides, prisoners usually only get to eat once a day."

"Don't be melodramatic, Sara; it's only for a month. And remember, your birthday is in a couple of weeks, maybe we can do something here for your birthday."

Sara just puffed through her nose in indignation as she rose from the table, "I'm going for a walk outside; in the woods."

"Okay, but be careful; watch for snakes."

Sara turned her head with surprise, "You know about the snakes?"

Jean smiled, "Of course. I did my homework before we even moved. That's why I'm staying close to the house unless your Dad is with me. I'll see you later." Jean smiled at Sara, but was met with a discontented glare.

"Yeah, I'll see ya later," Sara mumbled as she let the door close behind her.

Sara headed for the woods directly behind the house and realized a few steps from the back door that she had her tennis shoes on, not her hiking boots. But she wasn't going back in the house, not for now. She was too angry and shamed to go back so she just pressed on toward the edge of the woods.

Once she came to the deep underbrush marking the start of the woods, she turned and moved in the same direction she had gone a few days before. Her intent was to find the dry creek beds and explore along at least one of them.

It wasn't long before she came to the first one. She pulled back some of the brush, and after examining the ground for snakes, she stepped through and started a process of parting the brush, looking for snakes and then moving ahead a few steps.

Once she got past the heavy underbrush and in deeper under the tree canopy the brush thinned out and she was able to make more progress. The ground was more visible and she could easily see the leaf covered soil so she walked along the curving path of the creek bed. The terrain surrounding the creek bed was, at first, fairly angled so that she was traversing a slope. Sara stopped at one point and looked back and could not see anything but trees. The brush line and what she could see of the field at first, was no longer visible.

Sara thought to herself, *as long as I follow the creek bed I won't get lost. When I'm tired, I'll just turn around and follow it back out.* Sara moved forward and noticed that the ground under her feet was beginning to level out until she came to a point where the creek bed was barely visible. The area around her now was flat and looked like it would be a good place to camp.

Sara looked around and noticed a cluster of thick trees; smaller than the rest, but still fairly big so she moved over to them and sat down. Because of the heavy tree canopy there was very little direct light making it in to where Sara was sitting. She leaned her head back and closed her eyes. She felt relaxed and realized that her anger had dissipated. It was warm and yet, because of the shade, it was fairly comfortable.

Sara sat there for a short while deciding if she wanted to go back or not. She had no idea how long she had been gone, or how far she had come.

Sara opened her eyes and caught movement out of her peripheral. She looked over at a young man, perhaps her age, maybe a little older, leaning against one of the trees, picking at his fingernails with a knife.

But it was his clothing that puzzled Sara. He looked straight out of the Civil War. But what puzzled Sara the most was that he was wearing a Union uniform: dark blue jacket, gold buttons and the gray blue pants. Sara had heard that they held reenactments of the Civil War battles so she figured he was one of them and just trying to play a trick on her. Yet being the person she was, she stood and advanced herself a few paces toward the boy and addressed him with, "Hey there." The fact that he had a knife didn't faze Sara one bit. She was, after all, from Philly.

He did not look up, or at her; he just kept digging his fingers with his knife as if he were alone. That did not daunt Sara one bit. She walked right up to him, peered into his eyes and with a smile on her face, she stated once again, "You…boy, I'm talking to you. My name is Sara. Who are you?"

He paused at his task, looked at his hand, wiggled his fingers and as he sheathed his knife, he smiled, pulled his field hat from the top of his head and stated, "If your skin wasn't so pale white, I would peg you as an Indian from the manner you are attired."

The boy's statement caught her off guard which left her no choice but to answer with, "I beg your pardon. I'm not attired oddly. Now you, whoever you are, you're the one who looks the misfit. It's sweltering out on a July afternoon, and you're dressed with long pants, clumsy boots and a hat for heaven's sake."

"With all due respects, Miss, the females I have known, wore long dresses at all times of the year; up north or here. So I thought you might be an Indian because only natives expose their legs."

"Well, I'm not an Indian and these shorts I have on are proper attire for this time of year... And what is your name?"

"Oh Miss, I am so sorry. I am Jacob Wilcott. Just call me Jacob. That would be quite proper."

"I'm just curious, Jacob. Do you live around here? You don't possess a Southern accent. You sound like me and I'm not Southern."

"I do not belong here, Miss."

"Me neither, Jacob! This place is outsville and I'm not liking it one bit. So Jacob, where do you belong...if you don't mind me asking?"

"Not at all, Miss."

"Please, Jacob...just call me Sara."

Jacob smiled and stated, "Sara it is. And my tale of woe is a long one. Do you have the time to listen, Sara?"

"We'll make time, Jacob. It's still daylight and although it's hot out, we can sit in the shade. How about over there?"

Jacob shook his head in the negative and said, "Sara, follow me a few paces. There is something I must show you. This is important and there we can sit."

She followed along those few yards to another area of the clearing only to see four large moss covered stones in a line as if they had been placed there with purpose. Jacob pointed toward them and stated, "Look here."

Sara heard a voice cut out across the vast expanse of woods and it came from the direction of Sara's house. "Saaa-raaa," was hollered again and again until Sara, herself, faced toward where Jacob stood and began to explain that her brother was an annoyance, but...nothing! Jacob had disappeared!

Momentarily, and with her mouth gaped open, she stood motionless. Then she wrenched her head from side to side and frantically called out, "Jacob...Jacob! Where did you go? Where are you? This isn't funny! Show yourself at once!"

Yet, nothing: She began to cry. Her brother, Eddie, came trotting into that small clearing. Stopping just short of his sister, he asked, "Why are ya crying and whose Jacob? I don't see anybody... Come on, Mom's looking for ya."

Sara grabbed her brother by his shirt and said, "Hold on, Eddie. I want to examine these big rocks."

"What for, they're just rocks. Come on, Mom's waiting."

Sara bent down and ignored her brother while she rubbed her hand across each boulder, scraping off the moss. She eyed them closely, but saw nothing out of the ordinary, except each boulder had some marks etched on them. One straight slash, then the next had two and so on with the last one reading four slashes. She commented with a "Humm,"

This caused her brother to ask again, "Sara, whose Jacob? Was somebody here?"

Sara got off her knees and said, "I'm not really sure, Eddie. I don't know what to think; let's go see Mom... Eddie, don't say a word about this to Mom or anybody, okay?"

"Why?"

"Because I said, that's why." Sara looked at her brother with narrow dark eyes.

Eddie threw up his arms and said, "Okay, you got it. Mum's the word." They both made for home.

Chapter Six

Sara and Eddie made their way across the grassy field and as they got nearer to the house, Sara could see her mother standing on the back porch, her hands on her hips.

All the way, Eddie kept up a constant dialogue, "Boy, Mom is really mad at you, Sara. She has been worried since lunch when you didn't show up. Boy, you're really gonna get it; she is really mad. I haven't seen her this mad in a long time…"

Finally, Sara turned on her little brother, stopping him so abruptly that he bumped into her. "Eddie! I got it! Mom is mad, okay? Now shut up; I don't want to hear anymore!" They were about half way to the house.

As they got within range of her mother's voice, the tirade started, "Sara, what is going on with you. First you disregard all responsibility and keep us up half the night waiting for you to get home, and now this. Where have you been? I have been worried to death."

Sara walked up the back steps and past her mother. And as she walked by her mother, she mumbled, "Now who's being dramatic."

"What did you say, young lady?"

"Nothing, I just said I felt sick, you know, from the heat."

"Sara, you have been gone all day; do you realize that?"

"Mom, I got down in the woods... and it was so quiet, and I was so hot, I sat down for a while, and I guess I went to sleep. I didn't wake up until I heard Eddie." Sara glanced toward Eddie with a menacing look in her eyes.

"I called you for at least a half hour at lunch."

"Honest, Mom, I didn't hear you."

Jean paused for a moment and took a breath, letting her fright and her anger ease. After a moment she said more calmly, "Dinner is ready. Go get cleaned up. I imagine you need a shower after the hot day you've had."

Sara stood with her head down in shame, "Thanks, Mom." As she walked toward the front stairs, she stopped at the kitchen door, turning to her Mother, she said, "I am really sorry, Mom. I didn't mean to scare you."

"Go get cleaned up while I get dinner on the table."

At the dinner table, Sara's Dad asked, "Where did you go for so long today, Kitten? Your Mom was pretty worried.

"I just went exploring one of the dry creek beds that ramble through the woods and I found something pretty strange."

Eddie lifted his head, taking his mind off his dinner plate, and Sara shot him another menacing look. He once again looked down at his plate ignoring her glances and continued to eat.

"Strange? What does that mean?"

"I don't know, Dad. Just where the creek bed flattened out, and almost disappeared, I found four rocks all lined up in a row…"

"Well, maybe somebody else found that place and was just messing around."

"No, Dad, these rocks had slash marks on them and were covered with real thick moss."

"Maybe an animal clawed the rocks. There are wild cats around here; you know, bobcats and panthers, even bears. You better be careful by yourself. As a matter of fact, the next time you go why don't you take Eddie with you?"

Eddie looked up from his plate as Sara answered, "I'll think about it. But Dad, I go out there to be alone, and I certainly can't be alone if Eddie is with me; he never shuts up."

"Sara, that's not nice." Sara's mother broke in.

Sara looked at her mother, a slight tinge of shame to her expression, "It may not be nice, Mom, but it's true."

Eddie spoke up in his defense, "I'll be quiet, really, I will, Sara. I'd like to go with you."

With some insolence, Sara responded, "I'll think about it."

While Sara was washing the dinner dishes, the phone rang. "Sara, phone call; it's Tyler."

As she dried her hands, Sara took the phone from her mother, "Hello?"

"Hi Sara, Tyler here; how's things goin'?"

"Okay, how about you? Did you get your truck fixed?"

"Naw, that's gonna take me a few days. That mess of metal layin' in thu road was my transmission and drive line. It's gonna take me a few days to fix it."

"Oh."

"I was wonderin' if you wanna go to Wal-Mart with me nex Friday?"

"Uh, I don't think I'll be able to go anywhere until after school starts."

"What? How come? Geez, I couldn't hep that my truck broke down."

"Oh, it has nothing to do with you, Tyler. My folks got scared because I didn't call sooner. I'm the one they're mad at, not you."

"Can I come over and visit."

"I don't see why not; they just said I couldn't go anywhere with anyone. Say, my birthday is in a couple of weeks. My Mom and Dad said I could have a party. Maybe you could help me put together a guest list, you know, some of the kids that were at Wal-Mart the other night."

"Sure, I can hep you with that. I'd be glad to. How's bout I come over tomorrow, but I gotta work on my truck first? I'll call you before I come over."

"Okay, Tyler, I'll look forward to seeing you."

"Night, Sara."

"Goodnight, Tyler."

After Sara finished the dishes, she went up to her room, smiling all the way. *Maybe things won't be so bad, after all,* Sara thought to herself as she stepped lightly up the stairs.

Chapter Seven

The next morning after breakfast, Sara went to her mother, "Mom, if you don't care, Eddie and I are going to walk out to that dry creek bed and explore a little more. Is that okay?"

Jean stood there for a moment, "Sure, I guess so. Just don't be gone so long this time; don't make me worry, okay?"

Sara and Eddie both nodded their heads in agreement.

"And, for heaven's sake, watch for animals, snakes included," Jean smiled lightly, but then her expression turned serious, "and watch for anything else that might be a cause for concern."

"Sure, Mom, come on, Eddie, let's go."

Sara and Eddie headed out the back door and immediately made for the wood line at the back of the property. They followed the edge of the woods until they came to the dry creek bed and then ducked into the thick underbrush. All the while Eddie had been asking a continuous string of questions until finally Sara stopped and turned on him, "Eddie, what do you not understand about the concept of solitude?"

Eddie looked at his sister blankly and said, "Solitude, what's that?"

"That is what I like to have when I come out here." Sara leaned closely into Eddie's face, "It means quiet as in being alone. The only reason you are here right now is that Mom wouldn't have let me come by myself. So, for now, let's pretend we are alone."

Eddie looked around, "We are alone."

Sara sighed with exasperation, "Come on, but please; no talking. And if you have to talk, pretend like you're in a church and speak quietly." Sara moved ahead into the depths of the woods, following the creek bed until she came to the level location where she had seen Jacob the day before.

Sara stopped and looked at Eddie, "Now listen, I met a guy here yesterday; he was kind of a strange guy, not like the others I've met. His clothes were really old fashioned looking and the way he talked was different, too."

"They all talk different around here."

"Eddie, we're the ones who talk differently to them. Besides, that's what I'm talking about. Jacob did not have that southern drawl that most of them talk with around here; he sounded like us, like he was from somewhere up north.

"Anyway, I kinda got the feeling he lived somewhere close so I want to walk the edge of this flat clearing and see if we can find a trail leading away from here. A trail he might use to come and go.

"I want you to walk one way and I'll walk the other. Walk all the way around, that way we'll double check each other. And keep me in sight so we don't lose each other. I'll meet you back here."

"Okay. I'll holler at ya if I find anything."

"Thank you." Sara's patience was wearing thin, but she did appreciate her brother's help. She was curious how Jacob had disappeared so quickly the day before.

Sara moved out and away from Eddie, keeping him in sight. At the farthest point they were probably no more than a couple of hundred feet apart, but the trees were so dense that it could have been easy to lose him.

Half way around the level clearing they met and paused for a moment; both were hot and sweaty. Sara asked Eddie, "You seen anything yet?"

Eddie moved his head from side to side, too tired to even utter a word. Sara looked at her brother, "Your face is awfully red. We'd better go back when we meet at the beginning." The two separated and continued around the circle.

When they got back to the starting point Eddie plunked down on the ground and ran his arm across his forehead to wipe the sweat off.

"Come on, Eddie, let's head for home and get something to drink. You don't look so good." Sara reached down and grabbed her brother by the hand and pulled him to his feet and they headed back toward the field, and home, their mission unaccomplished.

When they got back to the house Jean was upstairs and when they came through the back door, Sara called out for her, "Mom, where are you, Eddie needs help."

Sara heard her Mom come rapidly down the stairs and then she heard her father's steps right behind. Jean rushed into the kitchen to find Eddie, sitting at the table, his arms folded on the table and his head on his arms.

"Good golly, Sara, what happened?" Jean rushed to the sink and drew a glass of water for Eddie to drink."

"We were just exploring, like we did yesterday, and Eddie started to get really red in the face, and then he got really tired; so tired he couldn't stand up, so we headed for home."

"Jack, let's get him upstairs and put him in a tub of cool water."

Jack picked up his son and carried him quickly up to the bathroom. Jean ran ahead and started the water running into the tub. Jack pulled Eddie's clothes off and when the boy was naked, his dad placed him down into the tub of water.

Eddie flinched slightly, but then relaxed as the cool water started to bring his body temperature down. Jack turned to

Jean, "I'll stay with him until he feels better."

Jean went back down to the kitchen where Sara was still standing, her face drained of color and a worried expression in her eyes. "Is Eddie going to be okay, Mom?"

"Yes, I'm sure he'll be alright." Jean placed her hand on Sara's shoulder, "Sara, that was very smart of you to bring Eddie back to the house. It could have been serious if he had stayed out in the heat much longer. It's very easy to get heat stroke in this kind of climate." Jean smiled warmly at Sara, "You did good, honey." She pulled Sara to her and hugged her tightly.

Jean pushed Sara back slightly, "Next time, take a backpack with some water and take breaks while you're hiking."

Sara looked sheepishly at her mother and nodded her head slightly.

Chapter Eight

Sara went up to her room and peeled off her sweaty clothes. After Eddie was out of the tub, Sara showered and then lay down on her bed and waited for Tyler to call.

Sara heard her mother's voice and it pulled her from a deep sleep. The hot weather had exhausted her and she had slept the entire afternoon. Sara heard her mother's voice again, "Sara, can you come help me with dinner?"

Sara slipped off her bed, stretched her arms and bent her back from side to side a few times and then called out to her Mom, "Coming."

After dinner Jean and Jack moved into the front room to watch a movie. Eddie returned directly to bed, where he had spent the whole afternoon, and was not seen for the rest of the evening.

After Sara finished the dishes, she walked into the front room and sat on the couch next to her mother, awaiting Tyler's phone call. The evening passed without that phone call ever coming.

When the movie was over Sara went up to her room and the more minutes that ticked by the angrier she got. *Now I know how Mom and Dad felt when I didn't call. I'm not worried that something has happened to Tyler, but the least he could do is call if he's not coming over.* Sara's thoughts ran this pattern and the longer she waited, the madder she got.

Finally she called out to her Mother, "Mom, I'm going to bed. IF Tyler should call tell him I've gone to bed; nothing more. Goodnight."

Sara slept fitfully that night, her anger getting the better of her. The next morning she didn't say much at the breakfast table, but seemed to be sulking; Tyler never called at all, not even late.

After breakfast, everyone scattered to do their own activities: Jack went up to his writing room, Eddie went to his room to read, Jean puttered around the kitchen, so Sara headed out the back door toward the woods grabbing her backpack she had prepared earlier.

"Sara, if you're going exploring, be careful. Don't be gone all day."

"I won't, Mom." Sara was not in a good mood. She was disappointed that Tyler had not called and now… she just wanted to be alone.

She headed out toward the creek bed and the stones hoping she would see Jacob again. Once she made her way into the trees and to the clearing, she looked around to see if there was any sign of Jacob. She sat down against a tree and drew out a bottle of water she had frozen the night before. By now it was melted, but still fairly cold so it refreshed her for the moment.

Sara leaned her head back and closed her eyes, the subtle sounds of the forest lulling her to sleep.

She awoke with a start. No reason why, there was no special sound or lack of sound. Maybe it was her internal alarm clock telling her it was time to head for home, but when she sat up and looked around she spotted Jacob standing in the same spot where she had seen him the first time.

Jacob was leaning against a tree slipping his hat band through his fingers, running it in a circle as if he was bored or waiting for someone.

"Jacob; how long have you been standing there?"

"Much longer than I would like, miss."

"Jacob; the name's Sara, remember?"

"Yes, miss, I remember."

"Then how about calling me by my name; it sounds so formal to keep calling me miss."

"As you wish, m… Sara."

"Jacob, I came by to see you yesterday, but you weren't here."

"I was here."

"But I called you… and you didn't answer."

"I was here nonetheless."

Sara paused for a moment, effected by Jacob's solemn attitude. "Jacob, you seem so serious, almost sad. Why?"

"Because I don't belong here; I am so far from home and my kin."

"Your kin, you mean your family."

"Aye, tis what I mean."

Sara paused once more, trying to figure out what it was about Jacob that just did not fit. Finally, she asked, "Where are you from, Jacob?"

"From Massachusetts."

"Massachusetts? Boy, you are a long way from home."

"That I am, Sara; a very long way."

"How did you get down here, I mean, geez, Massachusetts. I knew you sounded funny. Don't get me wrong, Jacob, it's nice to find another Yankee down here, but even I'm not from that far north."

"Where do you hale from, Sara?"

"Hale? That's a funny way to ask… anyway, my family just moved down here from Philadelphia, you know, Pennsylvania.

Well, actually we lived in a suburb of Philly, but we just moved here about a week ago. How long have you been here?"

Jacob was silent for a few minutes and Sara was afraid she had asked something more personal than Jacob was willing to discuss. Finally he looked at Sara and the sadness in his eyes was overwhelming.

"I'm sorry, Jacob, if I asked something that is too personal for you to talk about. I mean, if you don't want to tell..."

"It is not that I do not want to tell you, it is just that it has never worked well for me in the past."

Sara was getting confused. "Jacob, I don't understand, but I promise, I won't think badly of you if you've had trouble in your past."

"Tis not that my past is troubled, although it will be hard for you to understand."

"Please tell me, Jacob, I promise I won't judge you."

Jacob was silent for a long time and as Sara waited for him to respond she looked at his expression. His face was brooding, almost secretive, and she wondered what dark past he must have.

Jacob had been looking down at the ground until finally, he looked up at her and began, "My name is Jacob Wilcott, as I told you, and I was born in Stow, Massachusetts in... When I was twelve, I ran away to Boston where I signed on as a cabin boy on a sailing vessel. When war…"

Sara heard a voice calling. She turned away from Jacob to look in the direction of the voice and then she recognized Tyler's voice. "Tyler, in here; I'm in here. Follow the creek bed."

Sara turned around to Jacob, "Jac…" Jacob was gone. She looked all around her, trying to see if she could spot Jacob. He was nowhere to be seen. Sara turned back to where Tyler's voice was once again calling, "Sara, where are you?"

"Over here, Tyler." Sara stood up so that Tyler could see her.

"Whatcha doin' clear out here?"

Sara looked around again for Jacob then turned back to Tyler, "I come out here to sit in the quiet. You know, to think. I like the solitude."

"Oh." Tyler looked puzzled as if he did not understand the concept of solitude and Sara said to herself, *another one. What is it about guys, don't they understand about being by yourself and just thinking.*

"How'd you find me?"

"Yor mom told me where to find ya. I came over to apologize for last night and tell you why I didn't call."

"Come on; let's go back to the house." Sara turned to go, but then paused to look back one more time. She couldn't figure out how, or why, Jacob could disappear so quickly.

"What'cha lookin' for? " Tyler asked.

"Nothing, I guess. Just making sure I didn't leave anything."

She and Tyler broke out of the deep underbrush at the edge of the woods into the bright sunshine and immediately the heat was oppressive. They made their way back to Sara's house and were ready for the glass of iced tea Sara's mom had waiting.

"Thank you, Ma'am, for the sweet tea."

"Sweet tea?" Sara looked at Tyler like she did not understand.

"Well, that's what we call it here."

"But isn't it iced tea?"

"Well, yes, but unless you ask for unsweetened, it already has the sugar in it, and here, we like our tea sweet."

Jean smiled as she listened to Tyler talk, and then added, "So that's why when I ordered an ice tea the other day, they asked me if I wanted sweet or unsweetened. I always take sugar in mine so I asked for sweetened and it was so sweet I almost gagged."

Tyler laughed as he said, "Yeh, it can be purty sweet. When ordering out a lot of people order half and half; you know half sweet, half un-sweet. Makes it just about right; by the way,

Ma'am, this is just 'bout to my likin'." Tyler held up his glass and then took another lengthy draw on his tea.

"Would you like more, Tyler?"

"No thanks, Ma'am. But that shor hit the spot."

"Mom, Tyler's going to help me put together my guest list for my birthday party."

"That's nice of you, Tyler. Sara really doesn't know that many kids around here."

Sara looked at Tyler, "Maybe we can invite Jacob?"

Tyler and Jean looked at Sara, and almost at the same time, they each said, "Jacob who?"

Sara looked from face to face, and both of the faces had a blank unknowing expression. "Jacob Wilcott, I met him the other day in the woods, so he must live somewhere close. Don't you know him, Tyler?"

Tyler moved his head slowly from side to side, "Nah, don't know 'im. I know a Jacob Anderson, he's a senior at Ponce de Leon High School, but he don't live nowhere round here. He lives in the south part of thu district."

Sara did not say anything other than, "Oh," but her mind was whirling, *I wonder where Jacob lives, and the things he said today about running away when he was twelve... and talking about signing on a sailing vessel, and then he mentioned war. What in the world was he talking about?* Sara decided not to mention Jacob again until she could learn more so she quickly changed the subject, "Mom, Tyler and I are going to talk about the party."

That was a hint to Jean that they wanted to talk alone so Jean excused herself from the teens, "Well, I've got some things to do upstairs, so if you kids will excuse me. Sara, if you have any questions just holler." It was not lost on Jean that Sara changed the subject away from Jacob, whoever he was, but for now Jean would let it slide. But this was a subject she would catalogue for later.

By the end of the afternoon, Sara and Tyler had decided who she would invite to her party, and for the most part, the list consisted almost entirely of those teens that had been at Wal-Mart the past Friday night. Sara agreed with Tyler that everyone she met that night were really nice and would most likely accept her invitation.

August second, her birthday, was less than two weeks away, and fell on a Friday night before school started so everyone would be available to come. Tyler gave her the necessary phone numbers so that Sara could call everyone and issue an invitation.

Then Tyler asked, "You gonna invite that fella, Jacob?"

Sara hesitated for a moment, "I don't know. I'll ask him the next time I see him." Sara was confused. Everything about Jacob confused her.

Chapter Nine

The next morning, after breakfast, Sara looked at her mother, "Mom, I'm gonna go for a walk. You don't mind, do you?"

"Well, I thought we might go to a mall somewhere and go shopping for school clothes. We got rid of so much before we moved, that both you and Eddie need things."

The prospect of shopping got Sara's attention and the idea of talking to Jacob, as important as it seemed to Sara, suddenly took a back seat. "Oh, in that case, I'll stay here. When are we leaving?"

"Well, I have a few things to do here, first, but it shouldn't take more than an hour or so." Jean looked at the clock over the stove, "It's nine-thirty. Let's plan on leaving at eleven; we can stop for lunch somewhere and then we'll shop till we drop." Jean smiled at Sara.

Sara's face lit up for the first time since they had moved, "Sounds good, Mom. I'll be up in my room getting ready."

"Tell Eddie when you go upstairs; I think he's up in his room."

Sara took the stairs two at a time, happy and anxious to be going shopping. She stopped momentarily at her father's den and poked her head through the slightly opened door. She looked in to see her dad, his fingers flying across the keyboard, writing on his latest novel, "Morning, Dad; how's it going."

Jack typed a few more letters, and then paused, his fingers still held above the keyboard, "Morning, Kitten. Well, it's going. I get spurts of intelligible dialogue and then I have to pause to figure out where I'm going next." He smiled at Sara. "What're you up to today?"

"Mom's taking Eddie and me shopping for school clothes."

"Oh, that's right; she mentioned it earlier. Well, you have a fun day, and Sara? Don't break me while you're out there amongst the fashionistas, okay?"

Sara smiled at her father, "Wow, Dad, didn't know you had such hip vocabulary."

Jack smiled back, "Hey, we contemporary writers have to keep up with what's happening in the world and that includes vocabulary. Have a good day, Kitten."

"Thanks, Dad."

Sara continued on to her room, stopping briefly to tell Eddie of the upcoming shopping safari.

The day turned out to be one of the best since the Richardson's had arrived in Florida. Jean had asked some of the locals and they had suggested Panama City for the best opportunities for lunch and shopping. And other than the heat, it had seemed just like shopping in Philadelphia.

By late afternoon, actually more like early evening, they pulled into the driveway. Jack met them at the front door, "I'll bet you bought out the stores. Do we have any money left?"

"Dad, just wait until you see some of the neat things we found." Sara was excited to the point; she rushed past her father, loaded with bags and boxes, and went immediately up the stairs and to her room.

Jean followed Eddie in the door looking like she had fought the next World War. "You okay, honey?" Jack asked her.

Jean gave him a wan smile, "I'd forgotten how exhausting shopping, especially with teenagers, could be. I hope you've got dinner ready?"

Jack looked at her with a non-committal expression as she stopped in front of him, "Well, as a matter of fact, I've been writing almost all day…"

Jean slumped noticeably as the prospect of fixing food seemed to deflate her. "…until I stopped to fix some spaghetti sauce. Dinner is ready to set on the table."

Jack's face broke out in a mischievous smile as Jean seemed to inflate once again, "You're a doll. I knew not to believe all those things your friends told me about you."

Jean kissed Jack and then moved past him, dropping her armload of packages on the floor as she collapsed into the nearest chair, "Boy, am I glad to be home."

After they ate, Sara paraded one outfit after another before her father for his approval. At one point Jack turned to Jean, "Are they really wearing stuff like that now days?"

Jean nodded her head and whispered, "According to the girls in the stores, and the window displays, these are the latest styles."

Jack just raised his eyebrows and moved his head from side to side, "What is this world coming to?"

Jean just patted him on his back as she whispered, "She's growing up, Jack; nothing you can do about it." Jack just groaned.

The next day, after breakfast, Sara set out with the intentions of speaking with Jacob. Halfway across the field, Sara stopped as she heard her mother call from the back porch. She turned to see Eddie coming up fast.

Sara couldn't quite make out what her mother was saying, but it was evident when Eddie got close enough, "Mom says she wants you to let me come along."

Sara looked up toward her mother with a pleading expression knowing it was too far for her to see and then she looked back at Eddie, "Okay, but here's the deal. I want quiet;

solitude. Remember what that means?"

Eddie stood silently in front of Sara for just a moment, and then nodded his head.

"Well, aren't you going to answer?"

"I'm giving you your solitude."

Sara huffed out in exasperation, turned and then continued on toward the woods.

Once they reached the creek bed, Sara and Eddie turned in through the brush, and Sara noticed that a break in the brush was developing from the foot traffic coming and going at this point. It was becoming less difficult to get through the thick undergrowth.

She moved forward into the trees and the dark interior produced by the heavy overgrowth was a welcome relief from the harsh sun. The trees also seemed to cut the heavy humidity so that once they got far enough in, where the underbrush thinned out, it was a pleasant walk to the clearing.

Eddie was keeping true to his word and had not uttered a sound since he joined Sara mid-field. Sara would look behind her just to make sure he was still there. As they entered the clearing, Sara began to scan the interior looking for Jacob.

Eddie must have sensed she was looking for something and whispered to his sister, "Sara, whatcha lookin' for?"

Sara turned on him quickly and put her finger to her lips

as she shushed her brother, her menacing eyes telling him 'not a sound'. Eddie shrugged his shoulders and pulled his head in like a turtle, or at least that is what it seemed, until Sara turned back to her quest.

Sara did not dare to call Jacob for fear Eddie would make a big deal out of it so she just looked intensely around every tree. She even tried sitting at the tree where she had fallen asleep the other two times she had talked to Jacob, but this time it did no good; Jacob wasn't there.

After what seemed like a very long time waiting, Sara was getting restless and so was Eddie. He couldn't seem to stay in one place and kept wandering out away from the clearing.

"For heaven's sake, Eddie, will you please sit down? Why can't you just sit and rest for a while?"

"I didn't come out here to sit and rest. I could have done that at home. I want to explore."

"Well, I don't want you to explore. I'm afraid you'll get lost and then I'll take the heat for it. Just stay here for a while, will ya?" Sara's lack of patience was beginning to show. She was frustrated because Jacob wasn't there, and she really wanted to speak with him again.

Sara couldn't decide whether to leave or wait a little longer, but the decision was more or less made for her, when a sudden clap of thunder let her know that rain was just a few moments away.

Sara yelled at her brother as he came running, "Come on, Eddie, we gotta get to the house." Sara took off running with Eddie bringing up the rear.

Sara paused at the edge of the woods to let Eddie catch up and the thunder and lightning continued, some of them very near. Just as they entered the grassy field, the sky opened up. The two kids ran as fast as they could, as the heavy rain pelted them and before they were half way to the house they were already soaked.

As they got closer to the house, Sara could see her mother standing on the back porch waiting for them with towels in her hands.

Sara stopped to allow Eddie to catch up again and then took her brother's hand as they ran, Sara half pulling Eddie along until they finally reached the porch. As they ran up the steps they were laughing and groaning at the same time.

Eddie shook like a dog as Jean handed Sara a towel, "I was hoping you kids would make it back before the rain started. It got so black I thought you would realize what was about to happen."

"Mom, when you're under those trees, it's so dark you really can't tell what's happening out in the open. And besides, I'm not so sure we wouldn't have been better off staying deep in the trees. We might have stayed drier."

"Perhaps, but I'm glad you kids are back here. You just never know where the lightening is going to strike."

Jack had heard the kids come onto the porch and it had brought him down out of his den. Seeing the wet condition of the two, he said, "Did you kids just run across the field in this storm?"

Sara and Eddie both shook their heads up and down.

"Don't you know that an open field is not a good place to be in a thunderstorm?"

Sara moved her head back and forth and Eddie just stared blankly. "It's never smart to hide under a tree either," their father lectured.

"Well, gee Dad, what were we supposed to do? We were in under the trees and the only safety we knew was here, in the house." Sara looked at her father with a certain amount of remorse tinged with a little bit of indignation.

"The important thing is you're both safe, now let's get you dry." Go on up and change into some dry clothes.

Sara walked past her dad and went up to her room. After changing, she plugged her MP3 player into her ears and lay down on her bed. Before long she was asleep. Her dream took her back to the clearing.

* * *

Sara was sitting in the clearing and she turned and saw Jacob leaning against his favorite tree. He stood and walked over to where Sara was sitting and looked down at her, "I just want to go home, Sara; Please, I just want to go home."

Sara looked up into Jacob's face and the look in his eyes brought tears to hers, "I'll do what I can, Jacob; I promise."

Jacob nodded his head lightly, turned and walked away, fading into the surrounding trees. Sara sat there and watched him go, "I promise, Jacob," she whispered.

* * *

"Sara... dinner's ready." Sara jolted up and awake. Looking around, disoriented for just a few seconds, she realized she was in her bedroom. Her thoughts went to Jacob *I have got to talk to Jacob. I have got to find out what this is all about.*

Sara heard her mother call her name again, "Coming, Mom. Sara slipped off her bed and headed for the stairs and dinner, determined that the next day, she was going to get some answers.

Chapter Ten

Right after breakfast, Sara slipped out of the kitchen, her backpack loaded with bottled water and a sandwich. As she went through the back door, she leaned a note on the counter by the door, "Mom, went for a walk. I've got water and a sandwich so won't be back until after lunch. Please, don't send Eddie out looking for me. I want to be alone!"

Sara eased the door closed, then silently closed the screen door and took the back steps lightly. As she walked across the field, she kept looking back over her shoulder to make sure her Mom or Eddie weren't following.

Sara picked up speed until she was running towards the tree line and the dry creek bed. Reaching her entry point, she looked back one more time, and then, convinced that no one was following, she dipped into the thick brush and quickly moved under the heavy tree canopy.

Sara moved quickly along the path she had made and before long was entering the clearing. She walked over to the tree where she usually rested, set her pack down and sat down, leaning against the tree.

This time Sara was careful not to fall asleep. She wanted to make sure that Jacob wasn't some phantom of her dreams. She pulled a bottle of water out of her pack, unscrewed the cap and took a long slow drink. When she lowered the bottle she caught something out of the corner of her eye and turned to see Jacob leaning against his favorite tree.

"Hi, Jacob."

"Hello, Miss Sara."

"Miss Sara? Boy, aren't we formal."

"No Miss, just polite."

"Whatever... listen Jacob, I have'ta ask you some questions." Jacob nodded his head slightly. "Am I dreaming you? What I mean is, every time I see you I have been asleep, so, are you part of a dream? You never seem to show up when someone else is here."

Jacob looked at Sara, confusion and sadness mixed in his expression, "A dream; am I a dream? Well, not exactly, Miss Sara, but I am not of this world."

"What does that mean?"

"Perhaps I need to start over, Mi... Sara. As I told you before, I was born in Stow, Massachusetts..."

"Yes, I know and you ran away when you were twelve."

"Please, Sara, may I finish?" Sara nodded her head, embarrassed that she had interrupted. "I was born in Stow,

Massachusetts. My year of birth was 1848. When I was twelve I ran away to Boston and signed on as a cabin boy on a sailing vessel."

Sara was sitting patiently listening to Jacob until he spoke his birth year. Her eyes flew open wide and her mouth gaped open, but Jacob put up his hand to stop her from speaking, "Please, Miss Sara, let me finish… when war was declared, our sailing vessel was conscripted into the US Naval Fleet and I became a Union Sailor.

"In January, of 1861, our ship was sent out from Fort Monroe, Virginia on a secret mission to relieve Fort Pickens in the Pensacola Bay of Florida."

Sara was beginning to squirm where she sat, looking to Jacob, confused and troubled. She thought to herself, *this guy's nuts, he really gets into this reenactment stuff, either that or I've slipped into the Twilight Zone.*

"Please Miss Sara, let me finish and I will answer your questions."

Sara sat back against the tree and tried to listen to what Jacob had to say, but she was totally confused, either that or this guy was… well, he just wasn't all there.

"In February, a gale blew in and as we set sail to move out to sea to ride out the storm, I was washed overboard and ended up making shore near Fort Barrancas. I was soon absorbed into the infantry there.

I served there for over three years and it got really tough. We were surrounded by Johnny Reb and our only relief came by way of the sea. We were in enemy territory and we knew it.

"Food was coming hard to get until we got this here General who took command of the fort. He was a Hungarian fella, and not too well liked by the folks around the fort. He would send out foraging parties and they didn't like it none too well, cuz the general would use Negro troops. The local folks, those livin' around the fort, called all those Hungarian officers 'Foreners', 'Yankees' and 'nigger lovers'. They didn't take kindly to the Negro troops.

"Anyway, September of 1864, General Asboth, our commanding officer, put together a raiding party and we were to go to Marianna, Florida to disperse the scattered Rebel forces, to liberate any Union prisoners, and gather up horses and mules and any troops we could for the Union.

"Now this wasn't no expeditionary force. We had three battalions of the 2nd Maine Cavalry, one battalion of the First Florida Cavalry, and two companies mounted infantry from the 86th and the 82nd Regiments of U.S. Colored Infantry. I was part of the First Florida Cavalry. There was over seven hundred troops plus we had light artillery. This was no small raid.

"We moved out of Fort Barrancas on September 18, 1864 on the steamer *Lizzie Davis* until we reached the Eastern shore of the bay. We moved inland reaching a number of small farms, but not much resistance until we reached Marianna.

"There, we ran into some real heavy fire. During the

ensuing battle they fought us off and then the general, himself, led the charge and we took the town. During that charge, the general was wounded... and so was I.

"They took the general, and a few other officers, on ahead and got them back by ship, but me and the other soldiers, well, we had to go cross country by horseback.

"We made a couple of days riding, but then, we stopped here to water the horses; this here creek bed wasn't dry then. It was here that me and a few other fellas... well, we went to meet our maker. As I lay there dying I begged the boys to take me home. I didn't want to be buried in a strange place so far from my family and friends, but they couldn't help me. So I was buried here in a strange land far from home. But I wasn't content to stay here through eternity, so I remained here, in my present form, until I could find someone to help me get home. I am so lonely, Miss Sara, I just want to go home." Jacob looked at Sara with such a sad and lonely look in his eyes that Sara just wanted to hug him and tell him that everything would be alright.

Sara looked at Jacob with a sad heart and then she walked to where Jacob stood and reached out to wrap her arms around him, not totally understanding the situation, but when she did, her arms wrapped around nothing but air. Her arms went right through Jacob.

"Jacob, what is going on? I don't understand." She covered her face with her hands to try and hide from what she knew to be true; Jacob was a ghost.

She looked up into Jacob's sad and remorseful face, "I'm

sorry, Miss Sara. I'm afraid I have confused and bewildered you."

"Jacob, you're… you're…" Sara couldn't say the words.

"I am a spirit, that I confess, but I will not harm you. All I want is to go home."

"But…but…" Sara was beyond words until, "What am I supposed to do?" The girl was close to tears.

Jacob reached out a hand and touched Sara's face and to Sara, it felt like a soft breath had been breathed upon her and her heart went out to the young man. She looked at Jacob, his sadness now in her eyes, "Jacob, I don't know what to do… but I will figure something out."

"Thank you, Miss Sara. That is all that I can ask of you."

A quiet calm came over the clearing while the two stood facing each other until Sara asked, "Jacob, which marker is yours?"

Jacob walked over to the four rocks and stood over the one with three gashes scraped into the surface. "Here I lie, for much too long. I only wish to go home."

Chapter Eleven

Sara made her way back to the house, her mind reeling with the promise she had made to Jacob. *Where should she start? Who should she tell? Who could help her? And most of all, Sara, what are you doing and why are you doing it. Are you crazy? How can you possibly help this guy, I mean ghost, and why would you agree to this?* All these questions and many more plagued Sara until she finally made it to the house.

By that time Sara had figured out a few of the answers: *I want to do this because Jacob needs my help. Finally, I feel like someone needs me. And why am I going to do this? Because I know how he feels. I'm trapped here in this place and I have no one who can help me go home. Home to my real home in Pennsylvania. The home where I want to be. I finally have control of something and it has been a long time since I have had any control over my own life. If I could fly I would be gone in a nano second. But I can't fly so I am stuck here…just like Jacob. And besides, he looks so forlorn, so pitiful, and I feel like this is why I have been brought to this horrible place… just to help Jacob. I feel so sorry for him.*

Sara walked into the kitchen to find her mother hard at work preparing dinner. Looking around, Sara asked, "Is it time for dinner already?"

"Umhmm," her Mother answered, "Getting there." Noticing a strange tone to Sara's voice, Jean turned to look at her daughter. "What's the matter, honey; you don't sound like your normal self?"

"Nothing, mom… well, actually I've got a problem and I don't know what to do about it."

"Wanna talk about it?"

"I don't know, Mom; I'm not sure you'd understand."

"We used to be able to talk about things, you and I. Have things changed so drastically that we can't do that anymore?"

"No…" Sara hung her head trying to decide what to do. She wasn't sure if she should divulge everything to her mother, but it was too late now. "No, it's just that I'm not sure you'll believe me."

"Believe you? Sara, have you done something you shouldn't have?"

"No, Mom, of course not; besides, how could I? I can't go anywhere that you or Dad don't take me."

Jean tipped her head slightly sideways, "That's true. Well, then, what's the problem?"

"Can we sit down? I think it might be better." Sara sat at the table staring at her hands trying to find the right words to start with. "I might as well start at the beginning."

"That's always a good place to start."

Sara looked up at her Mother and Jean didn't like what she saw in Sara's eyes. The girl's eyes were troubled; very troubled. Sadness trickled from her eyes with every tear that now slithered down Sara's face and this alarmed Jean, "For heaven's sake, Sara, you're scaring me."

"I don't mean to, Mom, I'm just in a real mess."

"Okay, just start at the beginning, like you said."

Sara took a deep breath and began. She explained Jacob and their first meeting, and then their subsequent meetings until finally their last, just minutes before. Then she told her mother of her revelation of what Jacob was and then of Jacob's request to go home. It was this last statement that really brought on the waterworks. As the tears flowed freely, Sara cried, "Mom, I just don't know what to do or where to start. I just know that I must help Jacob get home, but I don't know how." Sara laid her head down on her now folded arms and sobbed freely.

Jean was stunned into silence. As Sara's story had unfolded Jean thought at first it was just a problem with another local friend, but then when Sara spoke of Jacob being a ghost, Jean didn't know what to think.

Then the realization that her daughter was meeting and speaking with phantoms sent Jean's mind into a whirlwind. She didn't know what to think, but she surely did not believe that her daughter was seeing ghosts.

Jean laid her hand onto Sara's head, "Sara," she whispered, "Let me talk to Daddy and we'll see if we can come up with something, okay?"

Sara lifted her head slightly and looked at her Mother through tear swollen eyes. Sniffing her nose, she muttered, "Okay."

"Why don't you go on up to your room and I'll call you when dinner is ready?"

"Okay."

Jean waited a few minutes to give Sara a chance to get into her room and then she walked slowly up the stairs and into the den, "Jack, we need to talk."

Jack was sitting at his computer staring at the screen when Jean walked through the door. He turned to look at her with a questioning expression, "My, you sound serious. What do we have to talk about?"

"Sara."

"What about her?"

Jean sat down in a nearby chair and looked at Jack, a serious and troubled expression all over her face.

"Oh, oh, must be bad."

"Jack, I think this move has affected her much more than we realize."

"What do you mean?"

"I just got done listening to the most fantastic story." Jean drew in a deep breath and then let it out slowly, "She told me that these long walks in the woods have been to talk with a ghost."

Jack's eyes flew open and his eyebrows almost hit his hairline, "A ghost?"

Jean threw her finger to her mouth and let out a "shhh" sound, "Not so loud, she'll hear you."

"Do you believe her?"

"What do you think?" Jean said with sarcasm, "Of course not!"

"Have you talked to Eddie; he's gone out there several times with her?"

"No, but I'll get him in here and we can both ask him."

When Eddie was sitting in the chair that Jean had vacated, he looked at his Dad, sitting at his computer, and his Mom, who was now leaning against a desk across the room, "Am I in trouble?"

Jack and Jean both smiled, "No, son, you're not in trouble," Jack answered.

"Is Sara in trouble?"

"No, but we do want to ask you a couple of questions,"

Jean spoke. Jean thought for a moment because she wanted to gain the necessary information without alarming Eddie, "Eddie, when you went along with Sara on your hikes together, where exactly did you go?"

"Just down that old dry creek bed, like we said."

"Did you see anyone else while you were there?"

Eddie shook his head back and forth, "Nope; nobody."

Jean looked at Jack with concern. "She did call for somebody, but there was never anyone else there, but just her and me, honest. Are you sure Sara's not in trouble?" Eddie finished up his 'testimony'.

"No, neither one of you is in trouble. We were just curious, that's all."

"Can I go now?"

"Yes, son, go ahead and go back to what you were doing."

Eddie went back to his room as Jean and Jack looked at each other, their concerns for their daughter fueling their thoughts.

Jean started the next discussion, "Jack, like I said before, I think this move has been more traumatic on Sara than we both realized. She has made up imaginary friends to console herself."

"We don't know that for certain; I mean, there could be a ghost."

"Jack, I'm serious! And you can't be; a ghost, really?"

"Well, I'd rather believe in a ghost than believe that my daughter has had a psychotic break from reality."

"Seriously, what are we going to do?"

"Right now, nothing; let's just keep an eye on her and see what happens. She's got her birthday party coming up. Maybe having a bunch of new friends around will bring her back to reality. And school starts within a few weeks, and that should help relieve her anxiety."

"Or make it worse. Remember, she's starting a new school in a new town and that is not an easy thing to do. That alone can cause anxiety."

"Look," Jack said, "Sara will already have a circle of friends, thanks to Tyler, when she starts school, so it should help ease things a little bit. Let's just take it easy and see what happens."

"Okay, but I don't want to be an ostrich and bury our head in the sand."

"They don't really do that, you know."

Jean looked at Jack with exasperation written all over her face, "You know what I mean."

"Yes, I do, and I'm not going to bury my head in the sand. This is my little girl we're talking about. Let's just give it a little time and see what happens."

Chapter Twelve

Once Sara was in her room, she plugged in her computer and hooked into the internet. On the search engine she typed in "Pensacola, FL Civil War"

After selecting a site, she read the information about Fort Barrancas and the sailing ships and then the Asboth raid on Marianna. And what she read sat her back in her seat. Everything that Jacob had told her was true, even down to the dates and the number of soldiers.

Although there was no way for her to determine the soldier's exact names, other than the officers, Sara had no doubt that what Jacob had lived, and died, was true.

Next she searched on line for Stow, Massachusetts. Many sites came up, but nothing gave her the information she needed. Next she searched for birth records in Stow, 1849, but still nothing was listed to her satisfaction. One notation did catch her eye as she read a footnote to one of the pages, *Due to the lack of organized birth and death records, family bibles were the only source of information at the time; therefore all records listed above are noted as to the family bible they were taken from and who now possess that bible.*

There were no names listed for Wilcott. Sara sighed with frustration. She leaned back in her chair and stared at the computer screen. She sat there for about ten minutes and then shut the computer down and lay down on her bed.

Her mind whirled with all the information or lack thereof and how she could possibly figure it all out. Soon she was asleep.

* * *

Sara's dream carried her back into the woods. She looked over and Jacob was leaning against his favorite tree only this time Sara noticed a difference. Jacob's eyes seemed much deeper set, almost as if they were sinking in and his eyes were surrounded with dark circles giving him a deathly quality. His face was bathed in sweat, his hair plastered to his forehead

Then Sara's eyes trailed down until they stopped just above Jacob's belt where a dark brown blotch darkened the dirty blue fabric, and then Sara looked again at his eyes and noticed that they had a feverish quality.

His head turned toward her and he reached his arm out to her, a beseeching expression, *Don't let me die here. Please don't leave me here. I just want to go home*. The words were not spoken yet Sara heard them as if they were.

Sara's eyes grew wide as she realized she was seeing Jacob when he died. "Jacob, I'm trying," Sara cried out.

* * *

"Sara, wake up!" Sara was being physically shaken, "Come on, Kitten, wake up!"

Sara opened her eyes to see her father standing over her shaking her. She looked around for a second or two and then lifted herself onto her elbows, "What happened, Dad; why are you shaking me like that?"

"You yelled out in your sleep; something about 'I'm trying'. What's got you so worked up, sweetie; did you have a nightmare?"

Sara thought for a moment, "Yeah, I guess so."

Jack had sat down on the side of the bed, "Sara, is there anything you want to talk about?"

Sara thought about it a moment, ready to seek help from her father, and then she lay back down and mumbled, "No, Dad; I'm okay."

"You sure? You know you can tell me anything."

"I know, Daddy. I'm okay."

Jack smiled at his daughter who was laying there before him, vulnerable to the world, yet so brave. Trying to be grown-up yet still his little girl, "Sweetie, you just remember, I've got a ready ear and an open mind anytime you want to talk."

"Thanks, Daddy."

Jack kissed Sara on the forehead and left the room. He met Jean coming up the stairs, "What's going on, Jack? I heard

Sara call out."

"She's fine; just a nightmare." Jack returned to his den as Jean said, "Dinner will be ready in thirty minutes."

Jean peeked through the door at her daughter who was still lying on the bed, with her eyes closed, but with a serious concerned expression on her face. Jean turned and went back down to the kitchen to finish dinner.

Later, at the dinner table, Sara sat quietly eating. Jack and Jean watched her as she sat, unresponsive to their conversation. When the phone rang, Sara, who usually was the first one out of their chair, just sat still. Jean answered the phone, "Hello,"

"Yes, Tyler, she's here, just hang on for a moment and I'll get her. Sara, Tyler would like to speak with you."

Sara didn't move or speak and Jack noticed that she seemed to be in deep thought. He reached over and touched her hand as he said, "Sara, Tyler's on the phone."

Sara jerked her head up, "Huh?"

"Tyler's on the phone."

Sara turned to see her mother holding the phone out toward her, a concerned expression troubling her eyes.

Sara took the phone from her mother and walked into the front room. Silence fell over the kitchen as Jack and Jean exchanged troubled glances.

Eddie looked around at everyone's faces, "What's goin' on; why's everybody so serious; and how come Sara's so zoned out?" He looked from his mother to his dad and then back again to his mother.

Jean looked up from her plate at Eddie, "Never you mind. You just pay attention to your own business." Her voice rang sharp and almost threatening.

Eddie looked like his mother had slapped him. He sat up like he had been shocked and his mouth fell open, "Golly, Mom, what'd I say?"

Jack looked at Jean with a shocked expression, "Was that necessary?"

Jean sat back in her chair and then leaned forward toward Eddie, "I'm sorry, son. I didn't mean to sound so sharp. I'm just a little worried about your sister."

"Why, what's wrong with her?"

Jean patted Eddie's hand, "Nothing for you to worry about, okay?"

Eddie shrugged his shoulders and resumed eating his dinner.

Sara returned to the kitchen, "Tyler's coming over for a while this evening. Is that okay?"

"That will be fine; we're just going to watch a movie

tonight. But Sara, next time, ask before you get off the phone; just in case."

"Oh, yeah, sure Mom; I wasn't thinking, sorry."

About an hour later, just as Sara was finishing the dishes, she heard Tyler's truck rumble into the yard. She dropped her dish towel on the counter and moved quickly toward the front door. Opening it, she saw Tyler climbing out of his truck, a big smile on his face.

"Oh, Tyler, you got your truck fixed," Sara exclaimed.

"Shor did, and boy, what a job that was; near broke me, too. Luckily, I was able to get the parts easy enough."

"Well, I'm glad you got it running. Why don't you come inside where it's a little cooler?"

Tyler offered his thanks as they walked into the house. Sara led the way into the kitchen and offered Tyler a chair at the table, "Would you like something to drink; some sweet tea?"

"Naw, thanks anyway; I just had some before I came over."

Sara had reverted into her serious and subdued demeanor and Tyler noticed right away that she just wasn't right. "Sara, what's goin' on? Why you so serious?"

Sara looked up at Tyler distractedly, "What?"

"I said, what's goin' on with you tonight?"

Sara came to her senses and looked at Tyler, embarrassed by her inattentiveness, "Oh, I'm sorry, Tyler. I've got a project I'm working on and I'm not having much success."

"Is it somethin' I can hep you with?"

"Probably not, I'm trying to do some research on the internet."

"Say, I'm purty good at that sorta theng."

Sara looked at Tyler, not believing that a country hick could be good at researching on the internet, and her expression gave her thoughts away.

Tyler looked at her with a big smile, "What'sa matter; you don't think a good ol' boy can figure out how to work a computer? I jus might surprise ya. Let me give it a try; where's yor computer?"

"Uhm, upstairs in my room."

"Oh... well, can we go up and use it?"

"Let me ask?"

Sara walked into the front room where her mom and dad were watching the television, "Mom, Dad, can Tyler and I go up to my room, and before you say no, let me explain. I've been distracted this evening because of some research I'm doing on the internet, and I'm not having much luck. Tyler said he could help me, and the only way he can do that is to go up to my room. Whatta' ya say; can we?"

Jean looked at Jack and he made a movement with his eyes and slightly nodded his head so Jean turned to Sara, "Okay, go ahead."

Sara called Tyler from the kitchen, "Come on, Tyler, they said it was okay." When Tyler was next to Sara she started to lead the way up the stairs when Jean called out, "Sara, leave your door open, please."

Sara's posture slumped slightly and she looked at Tyler and rolled her eyes. Then she looked at her mother, "Mom, really?"

"Sorry, kiddo, those are the rules."

Tyler smiled at Jean and Jack, "Ma'am, I am one to always follow the rules." The two teens disappeared up the stairs.

They turned the computer on and linked up with the internet, Tyler sitting at the keyboard and Sara next to her desk.

"Okay, now, what are we searching for?"

"I need to find out about someone who fought in the Civil War. I know when he was born and where, but I need verification and I can't seem to find any records of him."

"Well, the first thing is let's jus Google his name; what is it?"

Sara paused for a moment, afraid of what Tyler would

think, "His name is…" and Sara paused again, "Oh, shoot, I guess I'll go ahead and tell you. His name is Jacob Wilcott."

Tyler typed the name into the search panel and then paused, his hands hovering over the keys. He turned his head slowly and looked at Sara squarely in her eyes, "That name sounds very familiar. Ain't that thu guy you wanted to invite to your party?"

Sara tipped her head down, now looking at the desk, "Yes, but I can explain."

"Sara, are we looking for someone from the Civil War, or someone who is alive today?

Sara couldn't answer Tyler; she just sat there in silence staring at the desk. Then she mumbled something unintelligible.

"Wha'd you say?"

Sara was afraid to speak. She knew that Tyler would think she was crazy so she didn't say anything. Finally, Tyler turned from the computer and faced Sara, "Sara, what is going on? Are you making fun with me; cuz if you are I don' think it's very funny."

"The tears were beginning to gather in Sara's eyes when she looked up into Tyler's face, "Tyler, I am not making fun of you, but I am in a real bind. You are the only friend I have that I can turn to for help."

"How can I hep?"

Sara thought for a moment and then made a drastic decision, "Tyler, can you come back here tomorrow, in the afternoon, and then hopefully, I can explain everything to you?"

Tyler thought about it for a moment, "I s'ppose I can; I don't have anywhere's I gotta go tomorrow. What time you want me over here?"

Sara thought for a moment, "How about two. That should give me enough time."

"Time for what?"

"Never mind, I'll explain everything tomorrow."

Chapter Thirteen

The next morning, at breakfast Sara was not as distracted as the night before, but was still not herself. Jean looked at her daughter, "Tyler didn't stay very long last night. Did you two argue?"

Sara looked up from pushing her food around her plate, "What, oh, no; He's coming back this afternoon. We're going to work on my genealogy project more then."

"Oh, okay," Jean responded, not really sure what was going on, but glad that Sara was at least occupying her time with something.

"Mom, I'm going for a walk out back this morning," suddenly Sara turned toward Eddie, giving him her menacing glare "and I want to go by myself. Will that be okay? I'll be back long before Tyler gets here"

Jean thought about it for a few seconds and then shrugged her shoulders, "I guess that would be okay, just make sure you…"

"I know, watch for snakes. Mom, I always watch for

snakes, for cryin' out loud."

"Easy does it, Sara, keep yourself on my good side, okay?"

Sara tilted her head down, "Sorry, Mom."

"Eddie, we'll find something to do, so that you don't have to bother your sister."

Eddie perked up, thinking of all the possibilities for the morning.

After breakfast, Sara headed out the back door and for the wood line. Once she made it to the clearing she sat down by her cluster of trees. She sat for a few minutes waiting to see if Jacob would appear and when he didn't make his presence known she called, "Jacob, I know you're here. Would you please show yourself? I need to speak with you. Please, this is important."

Sara waited, leaning her head against the tree, but making sure she did not fall asleep. Then Sara heard a light whisper almost as if a soft breeze blew through the leaves overhead. Turning slightly, she saw Jacob standing by the row of rocks; the markers where his body lay, unidentified and unsanctified.

Sara stood and walked toward Jacob, "Good morning, miss."

With an air of frustration, "Jacob, what have I said about calling me miss; the name is Sara."

"I am sorry, mi.., I mean Sara. It is just that were I taught any other way I would call you Sara freely, but it is a common courtesy to call an unmarried woman, miss; You are unmarried?"

"Yes, Jacob, I am unmarried, I am only fifteen."

"But that is of an age to marry."

Sara huffed through her nose, "Jacob, that was then, this is now. Now listen, and this is very important to getting you home."

"Then I shall listen and not interrupt. Please speak freely."

Sara sighed and blew out a huge breath, "Okay, here's the deal. I have been searching on the internet for information, you know, birth records, that sort of stuff, and I'm not having much luck."

"But it was registered in my family's bible."

"Well, see, that's the problem. I haven't been able to find anyone by the name of Wilcott. Anyway, I have a friend of mine helping me and I really think I need you to talk to him."

"I do not believe that is a good idea, Sara."

"Well, I do! He knows a lot more about finding things on the internet than I do."

"What is this internet?"

"Never mind, now listen, Tyler is coming here with me this afternoon and I need you to appear and talk with him. He needs to know who and what we are dealing with. I need him to help me find your descendants so that we can get you home. Do you understand that?"

"Who is this person?"

"He's a friend and he has lived around here for a long time."

"Can he be trusted? What I mean is that if my bones are disturbed without the proper intention I could be lost forever. I would never get home."

"Jacob, he is helping me help you. He needs to see you so that he doesn't think I am crazy. If I tell him that a ghost told me what to do, he would help lock me away. So you have to show yourself to him and tell him what you told me the other day. Can you do that?"

Jacob had a serious, but sad expression and Sara could tell that he was considering her request. "Bring him here and I will do what I can."

"Thank you, Jacob. I know when he sees and talks to you then we can really start getting things set up to get you home."

"I hope so, Sara. I do wish to lie in peace in my proper home."

"Then I will be back in a few hours and when I get here I will call."

"I will know."

Later that afternoon Tyler arrived right on time. Sara took him into the kitchen and then told him to wait there for her return. Sara went upstairs where her mother was busy and asked, "Mom, Tyler's here and we're going for a walk if that's okay?"

"I suppose it will be okay; where are you going?"

"Out back into the woods."

Jean had been folding some clothes and stood up and looked at her daughter, "Sara, what is it about those woods that is so interesting?"

Sara stood there silently trying to figure out what to say without lying, "It's just quiet out there, Mom. A person can sit and talk without a lot of interruptions, that's all."

"Are you going to the same place; that clearing?"

Sara nodded her head, "Yeah, Mom, it's really nice out there. I wanted to show it to Tyler. He's never explored the woods this far down from his place."

"Okay," Jean shrugged her shoulders slightly, "Don't be gone all afternoon. Be home for dinner, at least, will you?"

"Sure, Mom," Sara went back down and led Tyler out the back door and toward the woods.

"Sara, where we goin'?"

"I want to show you something... and there's someone I want you to meet."

"Out here?" Tyler asked, amazed that there would be anyone out in these remote woods.

"Tyler, just follow me. It will all be explained in a little bit."

Tyler just followed behind Sara and when they reached the cut by the dry creek bed he noted that fact, "This is where you were before, ya know, when I found you out here thu last time."

"Umhmm," Sara kept moving while she still had the courage to go through with this.

Once they reached the clearing, Sara led the way over to the four stones. Tyler stopped a few steps back from where Sara stopped. The two teens stood there for about five minutes without a word being spoken. Finally Tyler asked, "Sara, what is going on? What are we doin' out here?"

Sara looked around, confident that Jacob would show himself and yet somewhat afraid of what would happen when he did. Finally, when Jacob had not come forward, she spoke his name, "Jacob, where are you?"

Not a sound was heard. Sara turned toward Tyler, smiled weakly and noticed that he had a very confused expression.

"Jacob, please, this is the guy I told you about this morning... Jacob, please show yourself; this is very important. Tyler is my best friend and he is going to help me get you home, but you must show yourself and tell him what you've told me."

Sara was getting frightened, not for any other reason than she didn't want Tyler to think she was nuts, "Jacob, please? You can trust him, honest." Now she was sounding more imploring.

Tyler took a couple of steps closer to Sara, "Sara, I don't know what's goin' on, but I think we better be goin back to yor house..."

Suddenly Tyler was staring into the angry face of Jacob who had appeared right in front of him. They were practically nose to nose. Tyler's eyes flew open as he reared back so suddenly that he stumbled a few steps backwards trying to catch his balance and finally tripped and ended up sitting on the ground.

Sara looked at Tyler and almost laughed; his eyes were so huge, so widely opened that she would have guessed that he'd seen a ghost. Oh, wait a minute, he did.

Tyler sat on the ground, his mouth opening and closing. Sara thought he looked like a fish out of water, but not a sound was uttered. And then there was his complexion; Tyler had lost all color. His complexion was white, almost ghostly.

Finally, Sara said, "Tyler, I would like you to meet Private Jacob Wilcott, sailor on the U.S. sailing vessel, Brooklyn, and later of the Florida First Cavalry, United States Army.

Tyler's mouth had stopped moving, but he remained staring at the specter that now stared down at him.

Sara stepped forward and reached her hand to give Tyler a hand up, "Sorry, Tyler, I didn't expect him to appear so suddenly. He's never done that before." Sara was smiling, almost chuckling, as Tyler took her hand and stood.

Tyler moved back a few steps away from the ghost of Jacob. He seemed confused as he looked to Sara and then to the apparition and then back at Sara. Finally, he looked at Sara, his eyes boring into hers, "Sara, I don't understand?"

Sara stared back at him, "Yes, you do, think about it, Tyler, just don't think too hard; don't let your mind be too rational."

Tyler stood there, his feet held to the ground by sheer fear and amazement. And by watching the expressions on Tyler's face, Sara could almost tell the thoughts going through his head. First there was doubt, then recognition, fear, denial, incredulousness, and then Tyler muttered, barely above a whisper, "This ain't real; he ain't real!"

Sara smiled broadly, "Exactly!"

"Exactly what?"

"He's not real; he's a ghost," Sara said, quite satisfied with herself.

"But Sara, ghosts aren't real."

"Tyler, if ghosts weren't real would we be seeing one?"

Tyler looked at Sara and then back at Jacob as the spirit slowly moved away from him and over to the four stones. Tyler was not cognizant of the fact that Jacob did not walk, but seemed to glide.

"Where's he goin'?" Tyler's voice was almost scared sounding.

"Over there is where he is buried. That's what this whole thing is about. Do you want me to explain or do you want Jacob to explain."

"No... no... you, you can explain."

Sara sat down at her usual tree while Tyler remained standing right where he was. "Tyler, why don't you sit and get comfortable while I tell you Jacob's story."

"No, that's okay: I'd just as soon stay standin' just in case."

"In case of what?"

"In case he goes crazy," Tyler motioned toward Jacob.

"Pul-lease, I've been out here several times. He's been a gentleman every time. If you want to stand, be my guest. So here's the deal..." Sara began to tell Tyler all that Jacob had told her and when she was finished Tyler was looking even more confused.

"So what are we supposed to do?"

"That's what I want to know? Where do we start and then what do we do?"

"Well, I'd guess that somehow we need to dig up his bones and git them buried up in Massachusetts. At least that's where I'd start. That oughtta git him home, don't cha think?"

"Tyler, we can't just box up the bones and send them through the mail to some cemetery in Massachusetts. There has got to be legal stuff, laws, you know. I'm not stupid, but there has got to be procedures to follow."

Tyler sat down and put his head in his hands, "Give me a minute to think. I still haven't processed all this stuff about a ghost."

Sara turned to Jacob, "Don't worry, Jacob, we'll figure something out; it's just going to take us some time."

Jacob nodded his head in understanding and then faded back into his grave. Tyler looked up just as Jacob faded away and stared at the apparition in disbelief, his mouth wide open.

Sara looked at her friend, "Well, if you had any doubts, that should take care of them. We are dealing with a bona fide ghost."

Tyler had turned very white, his tanned complexion now pale. His eyes were wide; very wide and Sara cocked her head to one side looking at him, trying to figure out why.

"Tyler, you have got to pull yourself together and help me figure this out.'

"Sara, let's go back to your house. I don' feel too well, and 'sides, we need to do some lookin' on the internet."

Sara turned toward Jacob's grave, "Jacob, I know you can hear me; we're going back to my house and work from there. I'll keep you up to date on what's happening. Come on, Tyler, let's go." Sara stood and moved toward the field and home, Tyler close, very close, behind her.

Back at her house, Sara led the way up to her bedroom. Walking past her mother in the kitchen, she said in passing, "Mom, Tyler and I are going up to use my computer, okay?"

By the time Jean realized what was going on, Sara and Tyler were already heading up the stairs, "Sara, leave your door open."

"Yes, Mother," Sara sighed heavily and rolled her eyes at Tyler. He just smiled.

In her room, Tyler sat to one side while Sara went at the computer with a vengeance, "First I'm going to the Stow, Massachusetts Historical Society; I was there before. After a few minutes she moved to another website and then another. Each time she was able to gain a little bit of new information hoping in the end that all the little bits would add up to the answers she was looking for.

After over an hour of searching, Sara heard her mother

call up the stairs, "Sara, I need to talk to you about your party."

"Okay, Mom, be right down." Turning to Tyler, Sara asked him, "Do you want to keep searching?"

"Nah, I think I know what we need to do."

Sara looked at Tyler quizzically, "And?"

Tyler sat there quietly for a moment and then answered, "From everthin' I've gathered from the websites we've been to I think the first step is to determine if Jacob has any living descendants. It's going to take their cooperation to make anything happen."

Now Sara was the one to look shocked. Her face drained of color and her mouth fell open, "Do you realize what that is going to take? Months; months and months of searching; I looked up on one site and the family records showed only Walcotts; not one Wilcott was listed."

"Well, as much as I don't want to talk to him again, we will need more information from Jacob."

"What kind of information?"

"For one thing the names of his mother and father. Over the years the family name may have been changed, maybe accidentally if not on purpose, so…"

Sara seemed to physically deflate, "Oh, no, this is just too much work. I'm too young to have to worry about this kind of stuff."

"Hey, you're the one who started this thing. I'll help ya all I can, but you're gonna have to follow through with this. Remember your promise to Jacob, and the last thing we need is to have him haunting us for the rest of our lives."

"Ooohhh," Sara dissolved into a moan and fell onto her bed.

"Saa- raa," Jean called from the first floor.

"Coming Mom."

Down in the kitchen Sara drew out a chair and sat heavily at the table. Tyler sat in another chair across from her. Jean sat down and then looked at Sara, "Look, your party is less than a week away. I need to know what kind of food to prepare and what we're having for drinks. I need to go shopping."

At the mention of drinks, Sara's eyes darted to Tyler with a pleading expression hoping he wouldn't mention beer.

So for the next hour the three sat there writing out a menu for the party. The calls had gone out and as far as she could tell, most of those who Sara had invited would be attending.

Her excitement was beginning to climb, dampened only by the heavy load of helping Jacob.

Chapter Fourteen

Friday arrived and Sara was nearly delirious with excitement. The party was scheduled to begin at seven, so all day, Sara and her mother were busy preparing food, while her father and Eddie were kept busy mowing the back yard area and setting up tables and chairs.

Tyler came over in the afternoon to help and spent the rest of the day and into the evening helping Jack and Eddie with the outdoors set-up.

Everyone ate a late lunch because Sara and her parents decided to barbecue hot dogs and hamburgers for the kids. By seven fifteen the first of the kids had arrived and Sara greeted each one and took them to the backyard where Jack and Tyler made sure they had drinks, sodas that is.

When Charlie arrived Sara introduced him to her parents as the guy that brought her home that night. They both thanked Charlie and then showed him to the backyard.

Accompanying Charlie were two girls, one, his girlfriend, Sherry, and another girl by the name of Courtney. Sara had briefly met both girls that first Friday night at the Wal-Mart parking lot. She hadn't really talked to either one of them very much, so she really didn't know them. After greeting the girls and thanking them for coming Sara had shown them the way to the backyard and then Sara and her mother continued doing things in the kitchen and talking.

"Sara, I notice most of these kids seem to be paired up."

"Yeah, seems so. I really didn't get a chance to learn all of the connections that first night because I had to leave so early, and then, well, you know the rest."

"I hope that you're not in any hurry to get… well, you know…"

"Mom, give me a break. Right now, I'm not 'planning' anything, and Tyler and I are just friends."

"Are you sure that's all it is?"

"Mom, please, no pressure. I'm not looking for a boy friend. Geez, give me a break, will ya," Sara sighed and rolled her eyes and then picked up a platter of sliced tomatoes, lettuce and pickles and headed for the door, "I'm taking these outside, okay?"

"Thanks, dear, and don't bother to come back in right away. Send Eddie instead. This is your party; I want you to enjoy it."

Sara stopped at the door and turned toward her mother, "Thanks, Mom." She threw her mother a loving smile and pushed the screen door open with her shoulder.

Sara stepped out the door and headed for the main table that was covered with various salads and condiments. After placing the platter on the table, she turned and searched the crowd for Tyler.

Tyler had taken over the grilling duties from her father and right away Sara noticed Courtney practically glued to Tyler's side. Sara walked over to the grill.

"Looks like you got stuck with the cooking."

"That's okay, I don' mind."

"Do you want me to help?"

"Shor, why don' ya get me a plate to put these burgers on."

As Sara turned to find a plate, she looked at Courtney and detected a look of anger in her eyes. Sara hesitated for just a fraction of a moment and then turned away. When she returned, Courtney had grasped hold of Tyler's arm.

"Tyler, I don't want you to get stuck here all night; why don't I go find my Dad?"

"Come on, Tyluh, les go fine Chaulie," Courtney whispered loudly, her southern drawl more syrupy than before.

Sara leaned back as if Courtney had slapped her, *boy, what did I do to her?* Sara's thoughts tried to figure out what she might have done to Courtney. Sara looked at the girl as she pulled Tyler away from the grill and toward some of the other kids.

As Courtney led Tyler away, she looked back over her shoulder at Sara, her smile one of self satisfaction, and then she turned away.

Sara saw very little of Tyler for the next hour as Courtney occupied his time entirely. Then when Sara's mother brought her cake out things changed.

As the cake with its candles ablaze was placed on the table and the kids gathered around to sing 'Happy Birthday', Tyler moved away from Courtney and stepped close to Sara. He smiled at the birthday girl as he sang the song along with the others and when Sara blew out the candles, he clapped along with the rest of the guests.

Sara was thrilled with the attention of her new found friends and smiled broadly as she looked around until she looked over at Courtney. What she saw in Courtney's face she didn't quite understand. The emotion was clear, but the reason was not.

Courtney's eyes were shooting daggers at Sara and she looked at Sara with such hatred that Sara was lost and once again her thoughts went to, *what did I do to her? Man, if looks could kill, I'd be dead, dead, dead!*

Later, after the party and the clean-up had begun, Tyler stayed to help. Courtney went home with Charlie and Sherry. At first, she wanted to stay and have Tyler take her home, but he insisted that she leave; he was staying and didn't know how late he was going to be.

So reluctantly, Courtney left with her friends and as she walked to Charlie's truck, she tried to drag Tyler along to say goodbye, but he pulled her hand lightly off his arm and just smiled at her as he said, "I guess I'll see ya at school next week, Courtney." Then Tyler turned away and went back to cleaning.

Sara watched Courtney's face and realized why she had been giving Sara the nasty looks all evening; Courtney was hung up on Tyler, and he either didn't know or didn't care.

A short while later, during the clean-up, Sara went to Tyler, "Tyler, what are we gonna do next about Jacob?"

"I got an uncle, my Uncle James, he's a rebel reenactor. I'm gonna talk to him about moving the grave."

"Well, don't give anything away, you know, like where it is. I don't want any one sneaking over there and chasing Jacob away."

"Oh, I won't. I'm jus' gonna ask him some questions, see if he knows any of the laws, ya know."

"Okay, I just know we sure aren't making any head way on the internet."

The next day Tyler paid his Uncle James a visit. When Tyler, in his truck, rumbled up into his uncle's yard, the man walked out of the house and met Tyler as he opened his door,

"Long time no see, son. Whar ya'll been?"

"Here and there, ya know how it is, Unc?"

"Why don't ya come on inside, sit for a spell. Ya want a beer?"

"No thanks, Uncle James, but I sure could use some information."

"Well, let 'er rip boy; I'll see if I can hep ya."

"I knows this is outta left field, but what do ya haf ta do to move a Civil War grave? I knows yor inta this Rebel Civil War stuff and I thought ya might know."

Tyler's uncle looked at the boy as if he had lost his mind, "What in thee world do ya need ta know that for?"

Tyler hemmed and hawed for a bit not really knowing what to say until he finally spoke, "Well, I found some grave markers out in some woods and I think they needs to be moved to a cemetery somewhere."

"First off, Boy, ya don't go an move a grave, specially some Civil War grave. Why, them Southern boys that died for the confederacy needs to be honored right where's they fell or where's they was buried. But ya don't dig it up and move it. Ya unnerstan?"

"Yessir, but this ain't no southern boy, this'n here is a Yankee grave."

"How do ya know it's a Yankee grave. Is there some sorta

marker sayin' so?"

"No sir, but…"

"No buts, Boy; ya don' move that grave. It jus ain't done. Don't ya even disturb thu remains. Ya put a marker there an maybe a flag, but ya don' dig up nothin' an ya certainly don't move thu grave. It jus ain' right an as a matter of fact, it's downright disrespectful."

"But Uncle James, if'n it is a Yankee wouldn't it be better if'n he was buried up North somewhere?"

"Son, unless you knows for a fact that the grave is a Yankee, and you have the cooperation of the family, thu grave can't be moved. But I'm tellin ya boy, it's got to be done with the right honors and dignity. Do ya unnerstand me, boy?"

"Yes sir, I unnerstand ya."

"Good, then no more be said 'bout it. How's yor Mama?"

Tyler spent another hour talking family matters with his uncle before finally leaving, but instead of going home he stopped by Sara's house. Once they were alone in the backyard where they could talk freely he told her what his Uncle James had said.

Sara looked at Tyler with a sad and pained expression, "Tyler, what are we going to do? I have to help Jacob."

Tyler just sat there solemnly moving his head back and forth. He was as uncertain as Sara where their next step lay.

Chapter Fifteen

It was the first day of school and Sara and Eddie were out in front of their house waiting for the bus by seven that morning.

The bus dropped Eddie off at the elementary school as it passed by on its way to the high school. When Sara arrived at her school, she went immediately to the office. Once there Sara told the secretary, standing behind the desk, her name and that she was a new student.

Jill had registered her shortly after their arrival in town and had brought them Sara's school records from her other school in Pennsylvania, but Sara had missed orientation, so she had no idea what classes she was taking or where she was going in the school.

The secretary mused about the situation for a moment and then asked, "Sara, have you made any friends that are currently students?"

Sara thought for a moment going through those she had met by way of Tyler and then a light went on, "Tyler Infinger; he lives just up the road from me. He's the first person I met here.

But he's a junior."

"That's aw' right, dear." The secretary stepped over to the microphone of the school's PA system, "Tyler Infinger, report to the school office."

Sara stood across the counter listening to the announcement, *Great. Now I'm going to embarrass Tyler by having him called to the office.*

Tyler stepped into the office with an anticipatory expression because he did not know what he had done to be called to the office. When he spotted Sara an immediate smile spread across his face canceling out the worried look he had, "Howdy, Sara, what's wrong?"

Sara looked at Tyler with an apologetic expression, but before she had a chance to speak, the secretary addressed Tyler, "Mr. Infinger, Sara says that you and she are acquaintances and she is unfamiliar with the layout of the school. For today, or until she becomes familiar with where her classes are located, I would like you to escort her around to each class and see that she gets there on time."

Tyler smiled broadly and then a frown crossed over his face, "But that will make me late fo…"

"I will write you a pass telling your teachers that you are assisting a new student."

Sara looked pleadingly at Tyler and then he said, "Shor, no problem Ms. Grouper, I'd be glad to hep her get to her classes."

Ms. Grouper, the secretary, handed Tyler Sara's schedule and the location to Sara's locker. Then she handed Sara the combination to the locker and the two teens turned and headed out the office door.

"Boy, you're a life saver, Tyler. I'm sure glad you agreed to help me."

Tyler smiled at Sara, "Hey, what awe friends fo… Come on, let's go this-a-way."

The two teens walked down the corridor heading for Sara's locker. The first bell had not yet rung, so the halls were still full of students, rushing in every direction like a wild flooding stream. Tyler and Sara elbowed and shouldered their way through the flowing current of students, until Tyler stopped and moved to one side, "Here's yor lockuh."

Sara stepped up to the lock, and referring to the paper in her hand, she moved the combination wheel this way and that until the loop of the lock gave way. Tyler referred to the paper he held and said, "Yaw'll need yo English book fo fust period and then yo social studies fo second."

Sara sorted through the glut of books she held in her arms and then placed the unnecessary ones in her locker. As she was finishing up, she heard a familiar voice, in that syrupy southern drawl, come from behind her opened locker door, "Why, hullo Tyleh, what's yo doin' down in thu Freshman area."

Sara closed her locker door and looked into Courtney's face, "He's helping me get to my classes for the next few days." Sara smiled a victorious smile, turned to Tyler and said, "I'm ready to go. See you around, Courtney."

Sara and Tyler turned away leaving Courtney staring at the backs of the two departing figures. Sara looked back over her shoulder watching Courtney literally deflate as an angry and vicious expression came over her face.

Sara looked up at Tyler, "Where do we go next?"

"Down this hall un then turn down to the right at the next hall. Yor home room is jus down a couple a doors."

Throughout that first day, even through lunch, Tyler and Sara were together. Tyler would see her to her class and then be waiting at the door to escort her to the next.

At lunch, seated with Tyler in the cafeteria, Sara spotted Courtney sitting at another table. As she took a bite of her sandwich she could see Courtney staring daggers at her. Several of the girls seated with Courtney would turn around and look at Sara and Tyler and then turn back and say something to Courtney and the dagger stares would intensify.

Sara didn't say or do anything to cause the dirty looks from Courtney other than she was with Tyler, but she didn't say anything to Courtney to ease her fears either.

Sara was growing a severe dislike for Courtney and anyone could see that the feeling was mutual. All the time, Tyler seemed oblivious to Courtney's feelings for him. Any onlooker could easily see what Sara evidently could not; Tyler only had eyes for Sara. For Tyler, at least, his and Sara's friendship was more than just that.

The first couple of days went well, aside from the dagger stares from Courtney. By Friday, Sara told Tyler, "I think on Monday, we'd probably better start winging this escort business."

Tyler looked at Sara with a befuddled expression, "Whatta ya mean?'

"I mean, I think I know my way around well enough that I won't need you to hold my hand."

Tyler took on a wounded expression, "Oh."

"I'm not being mean, Tyler. I've really enjoyed having you with me all the time, but I hate that you have had to take time away from your classes for me."

"Can we still meet fo lunch?"

"Absolutely; I would love to eat lunch with you. Then we can discuss what we are going to do about Jacob."

"Oh, yeah, I'd almos' forgotten Jacob."

"Forgotten Jacob? How could you?"

"Well, I've been so busy with school an' all. Say, Sara, can I pick you up and drive you to school. I'm driving my truck anyways an' I go right by yo house?"

Sara beamed, "Tyler, I'd love that."

"Yaw'll haft ta get yo momma to sign a note and yaw'll have ta turn it into the office."

"No problem, Tyler. My folks like you."

The next Monday morning when Tyler drove into the parking lot, Sara was sitting in the passenger seat. As they parked, Sara spotted Courtney staring at them and her eyes were large and livid. Sara just smiled at her.

Later that morning as Sara was retrieving books from her locker, the locker door slammed into her, hard.

Sara backed away from the locker rubbing her head as she moved the door out of the way. Behind the door stood Courtney, glaring daggers as usual, "Oh, excuse me, dawlin'" Courtney smiled a weak and phony smile at Sara. Then she turned and walked away.

Sara sighed and closed her locker. As she walked away her thoughts ran to what had just happened, *So that's how it's gonna be.*

The next day, Courtney was waiting off in an obscure corner of the parking lot where she could watch all of the incoming vehicles. As Tyler rolled down the aisle to find a place to park, Sara sat up a little bit straighter so that Courtney would be sure to see her.

Sara looked at Courtney whose eyes were minor slits, she was so angry. Later that day, in the cafeteria, as Tyler and Sara were eating and discussing what they were going to do about Jacob, Courtney walked up beside Tyler, "Hiyah, Tyluh; I haven' seen much of ya aroun'. Where ya been keepin' yo'rsef?"

Tyler turned his head just enough to see Courtney's face, "Oh, Hi Courtney." He turned back to his sandwich and then took a sip off his soda.

Sara didn't say anything; she just looked at Courtney and raised her eyebrows as if to say, 'sorry'.

Courtney's eyes immediately went to dagger piercing slits. She turned on her heels and walked back to the table where her friends were seated, watching the whole brush-off.

Sara turned her attentions back to Tyler, "Well, if we can't get anywhere over the internet, and we can't move the grave, then what the heck are we gonna do?"

"I don' know, but we'll figure out somethin'"

Sara looked at the wall clock, "It's almost time for class. I've got to go to my locker, so I'll meet you at your truck after school."

Tyler smiled, "Okay, see ya then."

Sara made her way back to her locker to leave her lunch bag and retrieve her afternoon books, when once again her open locker door smashed her in the head. This time Sara knew it wasn't an accident and she grabbed the door and pushed it hard against the aggressor, then she slammed the locker door.

Courtney was standing there holding her forehead, a surprised and pained look on her face. She aggressively stepped forward and pushed Sara hard, "You Yankee witch! Stay away from Tyler; he's mine!"

"Yours? He didn't look like he was yours when he brushed you off just a few minutes ago. Looks more to me like he barely knows you exist."

Courtney's eyes flew open and Sara was more convinced than ever that it was now open warfare. Sara turned on her heels and headed down the hall away from Courtney.

What Sara hadn't seen was the group of girls that were standing a short distance behind Courtney. They were her circle of friends and Sara had just embarrassed Courtney in front of them.

Courtney walked back to her friends, "That Yankee witch isn't gonna get away with this. I'll show her how we do things down here in the south."

Sara didn't mention anything to Tyler about her confrontation with Courtney nor did she mention anything about problems at school to her parents.

So when the next day's incident occurred, it came as a surprise to everyone.

After Sara arrived at school with Tyler she went to her locker and her morning classes. Sara was on guard for anything that Courtney might do, but by lunch, when nothing had occurred, she had started to relax and let her guard down a little.

When she went to her locker from the cafeteria to get ready for her afternoon classes she was not immediately ready for her locker door to come crashing into her head, but it didn't take her long to figure out what was happening and who was doing it.

So when Sara pushed back on her door and it smacked into something on the back side, just as before, she wasn't going to let Courtney recover. As soon as Sara slammed the locker door shut, she cocked her fist back and let it fly. She connected with Courtney's face just below her left eye. This reaction surprised Sara as much as it did Courtney.

Sara stepped back shaking her fist to relieve the pain in her hand from connecting with Courtney's face.

Courtney staggered back as her friends, standing back a few paces all gasped. Sara didn't see them or hear them. Her full attention was on Courtney.

Courtney staggered back holding both hands to her face and eye. Sara stood back bracing herself for what she surely felt would come, and it did. Courtney came flying at her, a vicious angry scream emanating from her as she charged Sara.

Sara leaned her head back as Courtney swung at her, missing the connection with Sara's face and then aimlessly flailing her arms. Sara grabbed for Courtney's hair and took her to the floor. Courtney was screaming and crying, spittle flying out and onto Sara. Both girls were rolling on the floor tearing at each other when one of the teachers came running up. The woman tried to pull the two girls apart before any other damage was done, but was physically unable to. Then one of the male teachers saw the commotion and came running.

Sara was now on top of Courtney pounding away when the teacher grabbed her by the waist and lifted her off and swung her away. He held Sara until she was able to calm down.

During that time, the other teacher helped Courtney up from the floor. Courtney was screaming and crying and tried to go after Sara, but the woman teacher held onto her. Other teachers had arrived and started to disperse the crowd of students that had gathered around the melee.

The teacher holding Sara told her to head for the office, all the while Sara kept protesting, "She started it...this harassment has been going on for days...I have the bumps on my head to prove it...this wasn't my fault...I was only defending myself."

By the time she and the teacher had reached the office, Sara was crying too. Just behind Sara, Courtney entered the office followed by the woman teacher and the school's resource officer.

The teacher that had escorted Sara had disappeared into the principal's office. The woman teacher then went into the principal's office while the resource officer stayed behind to prevent any further violence.

When the two teachers emerged from the office, they were followed by the principal himself. He walked over to the two girls, "I have called both of your parents and they are on their way. Once they arrive I will discuss with you girls and your parents exactly what happened and then decide what we're going to do about it."

The school nurse brought Courtney an icepack for her face and then they all waited for the parents to arrive.

A few minutes later Tyler walked through the office door and once inside he stopped and looked first at Courtney. The girl lowered the ice pack away from her face to show Tyler her wounds in an obvious move to gain his sympathy.

Then Tyler turned to Sara, a broad smile on his face. His smile quickly broke into a chuckle as he spoke, "Geeze, Sara, where'd you learn to hit like that?" His chuckle turned into full blown laughter as he turned and looked at Courtney once more.

Sara looked at Tyler and a small smile broke her tear stained face, "You forget, I've got a younger brother."

Tyler shook his head with understanding.

The office door opened again and Jean entered. She stopped in front of Sara, a look of surprise mixed with disappointment on her face. She turned and looked at Courtney and then turned back at Sara, her disappointment now masked by horror. "Sara," was all she said.

Sara hung her head with shame.

Jean walked over to the counter and spoke to the secretary, "I'm Mrs. Richardson, Sara's mother. I'd like to speak with the principal."

In the principal's office, Sara's mom introduced herself to Mr. Goodwin and they shook hands. "Mr. Goodwin, I am totally shocked about this. Sara has never been in any trouble before."

"I know, Mrs. Richardson, I have read Sara's school transcripts from her previous school in Pennsylvania and from all appearances she was a model student."

There was a momentary pause and then Mr. Goodwin spoke again, "Mrs. Richardson, this age is a critical point in a student's life and sometimes they don't take kindly to major moves. Have you noticed any changes in Sara since your move here?"

"As a matter of fact yes, she has been very moody and withdrawn. She's been spending a lot of time by herself taking walks into the woods behind our home. She was never like that at home in Pennsylvania."

"Has she made any friends here yet?"

"Yes, Tyler Infinger. He and Sara met right away and have become fast friends. Nothing romantic, Sara's too young for that. But they have spent a lot of time together since they met. And Tyler introduced her to a number of the other kids from around here.

"Sara recently celebrated her fifteenth birthday and we

held a party for her. Most of the kids who attended were kids that go to school right here. As a matter of fact, I remember the girl out in the office, the one with the ice pack on her face, was at the party.

"I just don't understand what is going on. This is not Sara. She doesn't fight. She would rather turn and walk away. I don't know what to say."

"Mrs. Richardson, the teen years are a difficult time, especially for girls. So many things are changing and one day you have a best friend and the next day they are your worst enemy.

"I'm not sure what started this dispute, but we have a low tolerance here on campus about fighting. After I have spoken to the girls involved I will make a decision, but no matter who started it, both girls will be suspended for a short period of time."

"But if Sara didn't start it..."

"I'm sorry Mrs. Richardson, but from what I already understand from witnesses, both girls were involved and that is the policy. You may take Sara home after I've had a chance to speak with her, so if you'd like to wait out in the office, I'll take care of that now."

"Certainly, I understand."

Jean walked out and sat next to Sara, "Your turn, and this better be good, because there is no excuse for fighting."

Sara tried to speak, but Jean held her hand up for silence,

"Tell it to him. We'll talk at home."

Mr. Goodwin was standing at the door to his office as Sara stood and walked through the door. Tyler had left to go to class leaving Courtney to suffer alone. The resource officer was behind the desk filling out some paper work.

Jean sat there, worrying about Sara, but at the same time she tried to look at Courtney's face yet avoid her eyes. Looking at the girl's face, Jean could only think about how angry Sara must have been, and that was not her Sara. What in the world could have caused Sara to be so angry and upset?

Suddenly the door of the office flew open and a woman about her own age barged through the door. Right away the woman dropped to her knees next to Courtney's chair.

Courtney had stopped crying a long time ago, but now the waterworks began in full force once again. The woman hugged Courtney, holding her tightly to her breast which made Jean all the more embarrassed. It was this woman's daughter that had taken the worst of the beating no matter who started it.

"Oh my baby," the woman wailed.

"Mommy, that girl..." and Courtney bawled all the more.

Jean looked at the two and her thoughts were not sympathetic, *this is no innocent. It takes two to tangle.*

Jean looked at the clock on the wall and realized that thirty minutes had gone by since Sara had gone into the principal's office. As Courtney and her mother continued their litany of tears, Mr. Goodwin's office door opened and Sara walked slowly out and sat next to her mother.

Mr. Goodwin signaled for Courtney's mother to come in to his office.

Once she had disappeared through the door, Courtney's tears ceased and the deadly glares began to be focused on Sara.

Jean turned to Sara, "Come on, Sara, we're going home."

Jean looked at the resource officer, "Tell Mr. Goodwin I will await his call."

Chapter Sixteen

The drive home had been a silent journey. Jean didn't ask any questions and Sara didn't volunteer any information.

At home, Sara had jumped from the car and sped immediately to her room, by-passing her father's study or any further conversation with her mother.

Once in her room, Sara had thrown herself on her bed and buried her face in the pillow. She didn't want to speak to anyone about what had happened at school. She knew eventually she would have to talk with her parents, but for now she just wanted to wallow in her misery. She was angry at everyone and the only way she knew to handle it was to be like an ostrich; bury her head in her pillow and hope that it would all go away.

* * *

Jacob was standing, looking at her, the most desperate and mournful expression she had seen yet. He was holding his hand out to her as if beseeching her to come to him.

* * *

Sara jolted awake. It took her a few seconds to realize that Jacob was only in her dream. But was he? She got off the bed, slipped on her hiking boots and made for the stairs.

Downstairs, she turned toward the kitchen and the back door. Passing her mother, standing at the kitchen sink where she was peeling potatoes, Sara said as she rushed by, "I'm going for a walk out back. I need to be alone for a while."

Jean didn't even have a chance to reply. She turned to greet her daughter coming from the dining room and then spun around and watched her bang the screen door as she left. Jean's hands were frozen in motion over the potato in her hands as she watched Sara go. Jean raised her eyebrows in surprise as she watched Sara disappear into the field behind the house.

Once Sara reached the woods and cut into them, she ducked in under the heavy foliage and made her way toward the flat area where Jacob was buried.

Once she reached the clearing, she called out, "Jacob? Jacob, where are you? Jacob, please, I need to speak to you."

Sara was turning in a slow circle as she looked everywhere for Jacob until finally she spotted him almost exactly where she had started looking.

"Sara, I am here. What is it you wish to speak to me about?"

Sara walked over to where Jacob stood, just above the four stones. She stopped and immediately plopped herself down, drawing her knees up practically to her chin. She looked up at Jacob and then laid her head on her knees and began to cry.

"Sara, why do you cry? What has happened to make you sad?"

Sara lifted her head and wiped her hands across her tear stained face, "Oh, Jacob, everything is just so wrong. I don't want to be here."

"Nor do I."

"I know, but you don't have a choice."

"Do you?"

Sara looked up at Jacob as her face clouded up again, "Ohhh, I hate it here! I just hate it." she dropped her head back onto her knees and bawled loud and long.

Jacob could not stand to see Sara sad, and lately he had grown quite fond of her, so the spirit sat down and wrapped his arms around her.

Sara didn't look up at Jacob, tears still clouding her vision. She couldn't feel Jacob's arms holding her, but rather felt a feeling of a warm and snuggly blanket engulfing her. She raised her head to look into the specter's eyes and felt twitters in her stomach that ran all the way to her heart.

She had a feeling like none she had ever felt before. Her heart felt large and almost as if it would burst. Looking into

Jacob's eyes she gently laid her head against his shoulder. It felt soft like lying against a feather pillow.

Sara closed her eyes and fell into a tender sleep. No dreams disturbed her, not even those of Courtney or the fight.

Sara sat up with a jolt. Looking around she realized that the clearing was beginning to grow dim, it was growing dark. "Jacob, I have to go.

She realized she had finally cried herself out and fallen asleep. She sat until the lingering sobs had subsided and then she looked up at the young man's ghost, "I'm sorry, Jacob."

"No need to apologize to me Sara. I understand your feelings. I do not really like it here either."

The two, spirit and friend, sat there in silence for several minutes and then Sara spoke, "Jacob, have you tried to get help before? I mean, am I the first person you sought help from?"

Jacob didn't speak for a moment and then quietly, almost in a whisper, he said, "Yes."

Sara looked troubled, "But why me, why now?"

"Because I felt you a kindred spirit; a displaced person. You were locked to this place just as I; a place you did not want to be."

"But how did you know?"

"I sensed it in you the first time you were here. But Sara, I must tell you. I will not be able to do this again."

"What do you mean?"

"This takes a great deal from me and it is making me weak. If you are not able to help me then I will be fated to spend eternity here, alone."

Now Sara was becoming alarmed, "You mean this is your only chance to get home...with me?"

Jacob nodded his head.

"Jacob, I have to tell you, I'm not having much luck. I have searched for family members still living in the Stow area and I'm not having much luck."

"I don't understand. Why should you need my family?"

Sara was getting exasperated, but tried to control her frustration, "Look, it's all very complicated. We have laws now and Tyler and I...well, we can't just dig up your bones and move them. We would get in a lot of trouble. It takes a family member to request the move. And even if we just dig you up, we still have to get your bones to Massachusetts and get them buried again."

Jacob lowered his head and moved a small step away from Sara turning slightly away from her as if he were giving up, already defeated.

"Look, Jacob, we haven't given up. Tyler and I, we'll keep trying, it's just gonna take more time than I thought, but we're gonna keep trying, I promise."

"I don't have much time."

"We'll work as quickly as we can. It's just that...well; it's just me and Tyler. We don't have any adults helping us so that limits a lot of what we can do."

"Sara, I was working a man's duties on a ship by the time I was thirteen."

Sara felt ashamed, "I know, Jacob, but those were different times. Travel is different now and there are a lot more people. Kids like me and Tyler, well... I hate to say it, but we're too young to be traveling by ourselves. People would wonder, you know, if we were runaways. Heck, I don't even know how to drive a car..."

Jacob looked at Sara, "What is a car?" His face was tightened up with confusion.

Sara thought about it for a moment, "It's too difficult to explain. Look, Jacob, I have a lot going on right now, but Tyler and I are going to do as much as we can as soon as we can, so please, don't give up.

"I promised you that I would help you get home, and by golly, I'm going to see you get home, no matter what!" Sara said that last statement with such conviction, she almost believed it, she just didn't know how.

"I have to get back to the house now, but I'll be back as soon as I can to keep you updated on what's going on, okay?"

Sara turned to go as Jacob responded, "I'll be waiting

right here."

Sara stopped, turned and then smiled at the ghost, "Why, Jacob, you almost made a joke."

Jacob never cracked a smile, but shrugged his shoulders lightly and then, as Sara watched, his solid form became a mist that then disappeared into the third rock from the end.

Sara stood, staring at the rock and then was overcome first by sadness, and then by utter panic. *How was she going to accomplish what she had promised? How was she going to get Jacob home? With her problems at school and then no help from the internet...how? Sara felt sorry for Jacob. She knew what it was like to feel misplaced and she had made a promise. A promise she felt she must keep, no matter how difficult.*

Sara headed for home.

Chapter Seventeen

When Sara reached the kitchen door she found her family sitting at the kitchen table eating dinner. Sara sat down at her place and spoke, her voice low and apologetic, "Sorry I'm late. I fell asleep."

Sara could see an intense expression on her mother's face. She looked over at her Dad and his was more a look of disappointment. That was when she knew for sure that they both were thinking of her episode at school that afternoon.

Sara looked over at her brother who had his face focused intently on his plate. Sara didn't want a confrontation at the table so she kept silent and began to eat her food. After a few minutes of absolutely no conversation, instead, a cloud of dread hovered over the table. Finally, Jean broke the silence, "Mr. Goodwin called while you were gone."

Sara stayed silent, but looked up and away from her plate and then looked at her mother.

"You have been suspended for one week…"

Sara sucked in making a loud gasping sound, "What

about my studies?"

"I'm going in tomorrow to pick up your books and your assignments." Jean watched as Sara's face relaxed slightly, and then added, "But you won't get credit for the work you do while you're out and when you return to school you have to meet with the school counselor."

"What for, I didn't start it," Sara said almost in a whine.

"Sara, those are the rules that Mr. Goodwin has handed down. They feel that you have some anger issues because of the move down here. And if it's any consolation, Courtney got suspended for ten days and has to meet with the counselor as well."

Sara dropped her head in submission knowing that it did no good to argue.

When her meal was finished, she asked to be excused and then went up to her room. The next week was spent doing her school work, helping her mom around the house and searching on the internet for information about moving a Civil War grave.

Tyler stopped by the day after the fight to commiserate with Sara. As they sat up in Sara's room, with the door open, they talked quietly about what had happened.

"Boy, Sara, I gotta tell ya, you and Courtney are the talk o' the school; too bad about getting suspended."

Sara looked directly at Tyler, "You know, this whole thing

is about you!"

"Me!" Tyler's eyes bugged out.

"Yes you! Courtney's got the hots for you and she thinks I'm butting into her romance."

"Yure kidden, aren't ya? Courtney an' I never been a pair. Heck, I just barely know her. Jus' from Friday nights, really, an' only since I got my truck. I never went before then. Why would she think I even liked her?"

"I don't know, but she outright told me to stay away from you, that you were hers! She's been harassing me for over a week."

"Man, I'm sorry Sara. If I'd known maybe I could'a put her straight before you got into a fight. You should'a tol' me."

"Well, maybe I should have, but that's all water under the bridge. Now I got a week's vacation and then I have to go talk with the school counselor. They think I've got anger issues."

"You, anger issues? Not hardly."

Sara smiled weakly at Tyler, thankful for his friendship. Tyler came by each day after school to share with Sara the gossip of the day until finally a week had passed and she could once again return to school.

Tuesday morning Tyler picked Sara up and when they pulled into the school parking lot Sara couldn't see Courtney anywhere. Sara left Tyler at the truck and said, "I'll see you at lunch. I have to check into the office before I go to class plus I have to see the school counselor sometime today.

Sara headed for the school office and once inside she made her presence known to the school secretary and then sat down to wait. Shortly after she took her seat Mr. Goodwin's office door opened and he stepped out, "Sara, would you come in please."

Sara stepped into the principal's office and was met by Mr. Goodwin sitting behind his desk, smiling at her, "Have a seat, Sara."

Sara sat and looked sheepishly at Mr. Goodwin.

"I hope you had a nice 'vacation'."

"I wouldn't exactly call it a vacation," Sara answered not intending to be insolent, but rather contrite.

"Hard way to get a vacation, I'd say," Mr. Goodwin answered Sara.

Sara nodded her head in agreement.

"Going forward, Sara, and I know that this whole episode was provoked by someone else, I hope that you will take someone, preferably an adult, into your confidence before the situation gets out of hand. Do you understand what I'm saying?"

"Yes sir."

"Good. Now this morning, during third period, you'll report to the counselor's office. After speaking with your mother last week, we both felt like it might be good if you could speak with someone other than your family about anything that might be bothering you. "Ms. Shawpach will be waiting. Okay?"

"Yes sir."

"Okay, Sara go on to your home room. Stop at the desk and get a slip just in case you run late."

Sara stood to leave, "Oh, and Sara," Mr. Goodwin smiled at her, "welcome back."

Sara smiled weakly at the principal, nodded her head slightly and walked out of the room.

At the end of her second period class, Sara stopped at the teacher's desk, "Excuse me Ms. Clark, can you tell me how to find the counselor's office?"

"Which one, Sara?"

"Ms. Shawpach."

Ms. Clark told Sara where the counselor's office was located and Sara headed for her appointment. Sara knocked on the door and was answered by a female voice that sounded young, light and cheery, "Come in." When Sara opened the door, she stepped into a very friendly atmosphere. Sara could feel it right away.

A young woman, seated behind a desk, looked up and smiled a very warm and friendly smile that traveled all the way across her face and into her eyes. Sara liked her right away.

"Sara Richardson, right?"

"Yes, ma'am."

"Please, call me Tina. I know it drops the respect level, but I really prefer to be on a first name basis, okay?"

Sara nodded her head.

"Take a seat, Sara."

Sara laid her books on a small table located next to a big arm chair and then sat down in the chair. She placed her hands, one on each arm of the chair and sat silently and waited until Tina was ready.

The counselor laid her pen down as she read the last few words on a paper in front of her. "Tell me, Sara, why you're here."

"Because I had a fight with another student."

"Yes, I know, but is there anything else bothering you?"

"No, not really." Sara had plenty bothering her, but she just didn't know how much she should divulge.

"Sara, do you mind if I ask you a few questions."

Sara moved her head from side to side indicating she didn't mind.

"Sara, do you like it here?"

Sara shrugged her shoulders and moved her head in a

wishy washy way, not saying yes and not saying no.

"You weren't happy about the move, were you?"

"No," Sara's answer was quiet, but firm.

"Can you tell me why?"

Sara sat quietly, still unsure about how much to say.

"Is it because of your friends; the ones you left behind?"

Sara looked directly into Ms. Shawpach's eyes, "We moved here because of my dad."

"Do you resent your parents because of the move?"

"No," Sara answered that question more firmly.

"Good, because sometimes we have to do things that are not always popular, but are necessary... Have you made any friends here, Sara?"

Sara perked up a little bit, "Yes, I met some of the kids, one in particular, almost right away."

"Who is the one particular friend?'

"His name is Tyler."

"Is that who the fight was over?"

"Yeah, but he's just a good friend, not my boyfriend. Courtney thinks that Tyler and I are... romantic, but that's not how it is."

"Do you wish it were 'that way'?"

"No! I have someone…" Sara stopped, realizing, for the first time, how she felt about Jacob. Sara also realized that what she was about to say, Tina would definitely not understand. She wasn't sure she understood it.

"What were you going to say, Sara. Please, feel free to tell me anything. Anything we say in this room is said in confidence. No one else will know, so please, go ahead and finish what you were going to say."

Sara just sat there staring at Tina, a scared look in her eyes almost as if a kid caught with their hand in a cookie jar. Sara clamped her lips shut tight and wiggled her head back and forth in a quick and jerky manner.

Tina looked at Sara with a sad and somewhat disappointed expression, "You're not going to say anymore are you?"

Sara tipped her head down looking at her lap and moved her head back and forth in a negative manor.

"Okay, but Sara, please if you are troubled by anything and need someone to talk to, please come and talk with me. I'll be here ready and willing to listen."

"Thank you, Tina."

"You may go on to your class. Here's a note telling your teacher where you've been." Tina handed a piece of paper to Sara as she stood to leave. "Remember what I said, Sara, I'm available anytime."

Sara turned and gave Ms. Shawpach a weak smile and left the room.

At lunch Sara sat with Tyler and never mentioned a word about meeting with her counselor. After school the two teens rode home together and when Sara walked into her house, she called out to her mother, "Mom, I'm home."

"Sara, come into the kitchen will you?"

Sara laid her books on the dining room table and stepped into the kitchen, "Hi Mom, did you want something?"

"How was school today?"

"Okay, I guess. At least it was quiet; Courtney isn't back yet." Sara reached for the loaf of bread to make herself a sandwich.

"Sara, a Ms. Shawpach called me this morning."

Sara stopped reaching for the peanut butter jar and turned to look at her mother, "What'd she say?"

"She said that she had spoken with you this morning and that you weren't very forthcoming."

Sara let her head drop slightly as she tried to figure out what to say, "I talked with her some. I just didn't have much to say about what she wanted to talk about."

"Well, she feels that you are repressing your feelings

about our move down here."

Sara started to object and opened her mouth to speak, but Jean held up her hand for silence, "She has suggested we take you to see a doctor in Panama City."

"A doctor! Mom, I'm not sick and I am not repressing my emotions… I just have a lot on my mind."

"That's the point, Sara. You're just barely fifteen and, other than boys, you shouldn't have that much on your mind. Your school work is fine; Sara, I just don't understand. Why all the alone time. You won't talk to me anymore, not like you used to. I'm worried, Honey."

Tears were trickling down Sara's cheeks as she looked at her mother, "Okay, I'll go, if you insist."

"I've talked it over with your Dad, and he agrees. We think you need to talk to someone who understands kids and the pressures they undergo. It won't be major surgery, just a conversation with the man, okay?"

Sara nodded her head in agreement.

"I'll call and make an appointment."

Chapter Eighteen

The Richardson family arrived at the office in Panama City fifteen minutes before Sara's appointment time. Sara stood looking at the door and the brass nameplate nailed just above her eye level. It read 'Robert Schiller, Doctor of Pediatric Psychiatry'.

Sara turned to look at her Mom and Dad, a downcast expression on her face. Jean just motioned with her head for Sara to go ahead and open the door as she put her hand on her daughter's shoulder. "It's going to be okay, Sara," Jean whispered in Sara's ear.

They entered the office and Jean walked to the receptionist's desk and told the woman of their presence. The receptionist handed her a clipboard with several papers that Jean then took to her chair to fill out.

About five minutes after Jean returned the clipboard, the receptionist stepped out a door and invited Sara in. Sara stood and turned to look at her mother and father, hoping for some sudden reprieve from this latest intrusion into her life.

Jean just looked at her with an encouraging smile and

Jack quietly said, "Just relax, Sara, the guy won't hurt you."

Sara walked through the door and then into an office. She stopped just inside the door when she realized she was alone. She looked around and then sat in a nice looking arm chair.

Shortly after Sara had seated herself, a man about her father's age stepped into the office through another door. He smiled warmly at Sara as he said, "Hello, Sara, I'm Dr. Schiller. I'm glad you took the initiative and sat down. I'll do the same and then we'll get started."

Dr. Schiller leaned back in his chair and looked off in a pensive manner and then asked, "So you're new to our area. When did your family move here?"

"In July."

"Where did you live before?"

"Pennsylvania, just outside of Philly."

"And you live in Ponce de Leon now?"

Sara moved her head up and down to indicate "yes".

"Boy, that's a bit of culture shock."

"If you only knew."

"Do you like your new home?"

"It's okay, nothing special."

"Have you met anyone your own age yet?"

"The first week I met a boy who lives just up the road. He's pretty nice. And then he took me to the local hangout and introduced me to a bunch of his friends. They seem okay, except one."

"Is that the one you fought with?"

"Yeah, but she started it."

"Do you know why she started it?"

"She's got this funny idea that I've got the hots for Tyler, that's the neighbor guy, but really, we're just friends. I tried to tell her that, but she wouldn't listen. Tyler's okay as a friend, but I'm just not interested in him as a boyfriend; you know, romantically and all. He's more like my older brother."

Dr. Schiller smiled at Sara's explanation and then he asked, "Do you have a boyfriend, Sara?"

"Well, yes, sorta."

"Sorta, what does that mean?"

Sara let out a huge sigh and she just knew that if she continued he would think she was nuts. "He's not real."

"You mean he is imaginary? You know Sara, we all at one time or another in our lives have imaginary friends. There's nothing wrong with it."

"That's not what I mean. I'm not making him up and he's

not imaginary…" Sara paused and thought about what she was saying. She surprised herself that she was saying anything at all, but for some reason, Dr. Schiller just seemed like the kind of person she could talk to.

"Why do you think he's not imaginary?"

"Because Tyler's seen him too."

Dr. Schiller sat without moving and Sara could almost see the wheels turning in his brain, "Sara can you explain what you've seen?"

Sara sat there knowing she had opened her mouth and was now about to put both feet in, "The guy I like… the one I called my boy friend… is a Civil War Union soldier." There, she said it.

"One you've seen in a history book."

Sara shook her head back and forth, "No, not in a book… in the woods."

"You mean a reenactor?"

"Huh uh."

"Can you explain to me a little bit more, Sara."

Sara dropped her hands into her lap in frustration, lifted her head and opened her mouth to speak, but stopped with no sound being uttered. "Oh, crud, I don't know where to start."

"How about starting at the beginning; that's always a good place to start."

So Sara went into a lengthy explanation of everything that had transpired since she first moved to Ponce de Leon. Sara watched the doctor's expressions waiting for the one that would indicate that he believed her to be crazy, but it never happened. She did notice, however, that at one point in her story, when she first mentioned the appearance of Jacob's ghost that Dr. Schiller's expression seemed to take on a more interested look. Not that he seemed to be bored, but she seemed to have piqued his interest. He became almost alert and from that point she seemed to have his undivided attention.

When Sara's tale had reached the present, she stopped, "And that's about it. Tyler's my friend, but I'm feeling something very special for Jacob and my moodiness has nothing to do with the move down here. I'm worried about how I'm going to help Jacob. I made him a promise and I mean to keep it."

The finality in Sara's last statement convinced Dr. Schiller that Sara was not going to be helped in the conventional way, "Sara, could I meet Jacob?"

"You mean you believe me?" Sara was dismayed that this man, a doctor, no less, believed her.

"Sara, there are many things in this world that we neither know about nor understand. The supernatural world is one of them. Ghosts, and their existence, have long been questioned yet not really proven or disproven. I have… a very open mind about the supernatural, even some experience with it, so I will repeat my question, may I meet Jacob."

Sara thought for a moment, "That will depend on Jacob. I'll have to ask him first and if he says yes, then I'll take you to see him."

"That sounds fair to me. Will you set up a meeting as soon as possible?"

Sara sat there looking at Dr. Schiller, "I thought you would think I was nuts, but you really believe me?"

"I think I do, Sara, but I'll keep my final judgment until I meet Jacob myself. Is that fair?"

Sara smiled and nodded her head, "Fair."

"Give me a call after you clear it with Jacob."

Sara's smile had spread all the way across her face, "I will; as soon as possible, thanks Dr. Schiller."

Sara had no sooner left his office than Dr. Schiller was on the phone, "Hello, Agatha, Dr. Schiller here. Do you remember me?"

"Of course, Dr. Schiller, how are you? Have you seen anyone from the other side recently?"

Dr. Schiller smiled at Agatha's question, "Not since Herr Hoffman, but I will be soon; that's why I called. Would you like to go with me?"

"Where is it that you are going?"

"Ponce de Leon, just a short drive from your neck of the woods."

"And why, Dr. Schiller are you going there?"

"I have a young patient who is developing a relationship with a young man's ghost, at least that is what I am supposing, and I thought you might like to go and visit with him. You are so much more adept at speaking to the spirits."

"Come now, Dr. Schiller, I feel you are quite competent at dealing with those from the other side. Do you know any specifics?"

"What I know is that he is a young Union Civil War soldier originally from Massachusetts who was buried at a remote location in the woods in Ponce de Leon and he has appeared to my patient in a plea to be taken home. He wants to go home."

"Well, Dr. Schiller, that is very reasonable. He cannot cross over until his needs are met. In this case his needs require the reburial of his remains in Massachusetts. Until that is done, he will remain a spirit of this earthly plane. He must be moved."

"Agatha, would you like to go with me to meet this young man?"

"Oh, as much as I would, Dr. Schiller, I don't think I could make the walk. My legs just aren't what they used to be and in the woods, I'm sure the footing would be tenuous at best, so as much as I would like to speak with this young man, the responsibility will have to be placed on your shoulders."

"I appreciate you taking time to talk with me, but I really must go. I have a patient I must tend to, but I will follow up and give you a call after I meet him. Thank you for talking with me."

"My pleasure, Dr. Schiller. Please do call me back. And, good luck, Dr. Schiller. Good bye."

Dr. Schiller placed the receiver on the cradle more determined to help Sara and her 'Yankee Boy' than ever.

Chapter Nineteen

After Sara's session with Dr. Schiller, he told her parents that he needed to do some research and would get back to them.

The next day after school, Sara came down from her room and moved toward the back door, "Where're you going, Sara?"

"Just for a walk, Dr. Schiller didn't say I couldn't take my walks."

"Okay, just don't forget dinner time."

"Okay," Sara headed out the back door moving off toward the woods.

Just as the back door screen slammed shut, Eddie bounded into the kitchen, "Where's Sara going, Mom?"

"For a walk."

"Can I go with her?"

"I think you'd better let her have some time alone.

Maybe next time, besides, don't you have some homework?"

Eddie hung his head, "Yeah."

"Then get to it, Son."

As Eddie headed back up to his room the phone rang, "Hello?" Jean answered.

"Mrs. Richardson, this is Dr. Schiller."

"Yes, Dr. Schiller, what can I do for you?"

"Mrs. Richardson, after my conversation with Sara yesterday I have consulted some books and read up on a few things about what might be affecting Sara. I had a few more questions I needed to ask her. Is she there?"

"No, she's gone for a walk out to the woods. She said that you told her it would be good for her?"

"Yes, yes, quite correct. When she returns would you please have her call me. I'll give you my cell phone number in case it is after office hours."

"Of course, Dr. Schiller… if I might pry, but is Sara… Oh, I don't know how to ask the question without sounding doomsday."

"Is she crazy? Certainly not, but she has confided in me some things that I find quite out of the ordinary that I hope to soon either prove or disprove. Please have her call me when she gets back."

"Of course, doctor, I will."

"Thank you, Mrs. Richardson."

When Sara had reached the clearing she moved to the four rocks and sat down near her favorite tree, "Jacob, I need to speak with you."

Within seconds she heard a reply, "I am here. What would you speak to me of?"

Rather than depressed as she usually was when she visited Jacob, Sara was more uplifted today, "Jacob, I have some wonderful news."

Jacob sat down next to Sara and looked into her eyes, "You seem in much better spirits than last I saw you."

Sara smiled, "Wait until I tell you of my news. I have met a man, an adult, who believed me when I mentioned you. I don't know why, but I believe this man can help us get you home."

"Has he said such?"

"Well, no, but he didn't think I was crazy when I mentioned meeting a ghost, and as a matter of fact…" Sara paused knowing that her request was going to meet with some resistance, "he wants to meet you."

The specter of Jacob sat more upright, "Why must he meet me?"

"For one thing to prove that I am not imagining you."

"But you are not imagining me. I am real."

"No, Jacob, you aren't; you're a ghost. In our world most people don't believe in ghosts and this guy is at least willing to give me the benefit of the doubt. Besides, if you will meet him, he might be able to help us get you home. An adult can move around more freely than someone my age."

"If it will help, and I must, then I will meet with him."

Sara let out a squeal, "Oh, Jacob, I'm so glad. You don't know how glad I am. With his help we might be able to get this show on the road."

"Show on the road?" Jacob looked around in all directions, "I do not see any minstrel players. Sara, I don't understand."

"Never mind, oh, Jacob, I am so happy." Sara reached out to hug Jacob and her arms went through a mist, making contact with nothing. She pulled back to see that Jacob had disappeared. She looked around to see if he had moved and spotted a glimpse of color off through the trees. Then Sara heard the sound of voices and of foot fall through the brush.

Sara stood still as two men came crashing through the underbrush just before they entered into the clearing. Sara stood there, aghast at the sight of someone else entering hers and Jacob's private domain.

Once the men were close enough they spotted Sara and

moved toward her. "Hi, what are you doing way out here in the middle of nowhere?" one of them asked.

"I live that way. I come out here to be alone. Who are you guys?"

"Surveyors. We're plotting out a development that will be coming here within a few months."

"Development? What kind of development?"

"Housing, a fairly major one to be exact."

"Here? In Ponce de Leon? This is all farming country. Why would someone want to build a housing development way out here?"

"For the country life; each lot will be approximately two acres with a nice custom house. This development will be for people who want to have horses. Shoot, a couple of months from now there will be bulldozers all over the place, clearing out all of this underbrush and trees."

"Bulldozers?" Sara said with astonishment that was quickly turning to fright, "Here? Right here?"

"Yes, miss. Shoot, within a year you'll have a whole bunch of new neighbors."

"Bulldozers will come in right here?"

"Yup; right here. The developer wants to get rid of all the weedy type growth and put in better looking trees. Heck, maybe even a palm or two."

Sara looked toward the four rocks and thought, *this will all be buried and then Jacob will be lost forever. We've got to act now.* "Thanks, guys, I gotta go, time for my dinner."

The two guys looked at their watches and then looked at Sara with a questioning gaze.

"I mean supper. I'm from up north and I haven't gotten used to all the proper words yet. See ya." Sara turned on her heels and fled the clearing heading for home.

When she came through the back door, Eddie was setting the table for dinner, "Eddie, where's Mom?"

"Upstairs talking to Dad, why?"

Sara sped past her brother and headed up the stairs. She knocked lightly on the door to her father's study, "Mom, Dad, can I come in?"

"Come on in, Sara."

Sara opened the door, "You guys are never gonna guess what's going on in the woods."

"Sara, you need to call Dr. Schiller right away."

With Sara's mind going miles an hour about the new development and what it meant for Jacob, her mother's statement caught her off guard and stopped her momentum, "Oh, okay, I'll call him right now."

Sara placed the call, catching Dr. Schiller just as he was about to leave his office, "Dr. Schiller, Jacob has agreed to meet you, but there is another wrinkle in this whole thing."

"What is that, Sara?"

"I ran into some surveyors today, and the place in the woods where Jacob is buried is about to be plowed under. A new housing development is going in and… and if that happens…" Sara started to cry."

"Sara, take a deep breath and try to calm down, then finish."

Sara inhaled deeply and let the air out slowly, "Dr. Schiller, if that happens Jacob will be lost forever." Now Sara was really crying.

"Sara, day after tomorrow is Saturday. Suppose I come up there and you take me out to meet Jacob. Once I've met him then we'll discuss the next move. Okay?"

"Okay," Sara managed to say between sobs, "but we've got to hurry."

"See you Saturday, Sara."

"Good night Dr. Schiller."

Chapter Twenty

Saturday couldn't come soon enough for Sara. At school Friday, she told Tyler of the development and of Dr. Schiller's impending visit. "Do you want me there?" Tyler asked Sara.

"No, that's okay. I can handle it, but I'll let you know on Monday what happens."

When Dr. Schiller arrived at the Richardson home, Jean was taken aback, "Hello, Dr. Schiller, I didn't know doctors made house calls, especially psychiatrists."

Dr. Schiller smiled at Jean, a rather guilty tone to his smile, "Well, normally I don't, but this is a rather peculiar circumstance. Didn't Sara mention that I was coming?"

"No, she didn't." Jean then called Sara down from her room. When Sara saw Dr. Schiller waiting just inside the front door, she called out to him from the stairs, "Hi, Dr. Schiller, Ready to take a walk?"

Jean looked from Sara to Dr. Schiller, "Have I missed something?" she asked the doctor.

Once again he took on a sheepish grin, "I felt that it

might be good if I investigated Sara's 'friend' myself, so she's taking me for a walk out to the woods."

"Friend? What friend?"

Now Sara took on a sheepish expression. "I guess I've never mentioned him."

"Him? Who him? Would you please explain what you are talking about, Sara?"

"Look, Mom, my friend is out in the woods where I like to go. Why don't you come with us? Then you'll know that I'm not crazy. Will that be okay Dr. Schiller?"

"By all means, I think it would be a good idea."

As the threesome was heading out the back door, Eddie happened into the kitchen, "Where's everybody goin'?"

"For a walk," Sara answered.

"Can I come along?"

Sara turned to her mother with a deathly look in her eyes, "Mom, can't you do something? Jacob isn't expecting a whole party, just Dr. Schiller."

"Eddie, I don't think…"

"Oh please, Mom, I've been out there before."

Jean looked at Sara and then at Dr. Schiller, who then shrugged his shoulders. Then she replied to Eddie, "Okay, but on one condition — no talking, no questions. You follow behind and don't say a word, okay?"

Eddie ran his fingers across his mouth as if he were zipping it shut and nodded his head. The foursome then headed toward the woods.

As they approached the cut into the trees Sara motioned that here was where they would move in under the tree canopy. The group moved soundlessly, no one saying anything and their footfalls making very little noise.

Once they reached the clearing they stopped just behind Sara. She motioned for them to stay where they were as she moved over to her tree near the stones.

Looking back at the others, she turned and softly said, "Jacob, are you here? It's Sara."

When Jacob didn't appear she spoke again, "Jacob, I know there are more people here than you expected, but I couldn't help it. Dr. Schiller is here as I said, and one is my mother and the other is my little brother, Eddie. You've seen him before, he's just never seen you."

Sara turned to look apologetically at the others and then saw her mother's eyes go wide. Eddie's eyes got round and he went pale, but it was Dr. Schiller who's reaction Sara found amazing. His eyes took on a wondrous expression and a slow smile crept over his face. Sara turned back toward the stones knowing who, or what, she would see. "Hello, Jacob."

Jacob's ghost moved a couple of steps closer to Sara as she smiled at him, "Hello Sara, I am pleased that you are here."

Sara turned back toward her mother and Dr. Schiller and motioned the group forward, "Jacob, this is Dr. Schiller. He's the one I think may be able to help us."

Dr. Schiller nodded his head forward in greeting, "How do you do, young man."

"I am not well as I have a veritable quandary, sir."

"I understand. I hope that I may help."

"I hope as much as well."

Sara looked back at her mother who had not moved, but had gone pale from fright. "Mom, this is Jacob Wilcott."

Jean stood frozen to the ground under her feet; unable to move forward or backward. Her mouth hung open and small sounds seemed to be gurgling up her throat and out her mouth, but they could not have been mistaken as words.

"Mom, wake up! Mom! Earth to Mom!" Sara looked to Dr. Schiller, her own eyes wide as saucers, "What's wrong with her, Dr. Schiller?"

"I don't think she was quite prepared for meeting Jacob." Dr. Schiller walked back to Jean, removing something from his pocket. He snapped the article and then waved it under Jean's nose.

Jean reared back and her eyes flew wider yet and then she stepped back, coughing slightly.

"Mrs. Richardson, wake up!"

"I am awake, Dr. Schiller, or at least I think I am. I'm just not sure of what I 'm seeing right now."

"What you are seeing, Mrs. Richardson, is an apparition. A ghost, if you will."

"A gh...gh...ghost?"

"Yes." Dr. Schiller said with firmness.

Then he looked to Eddie who had moved closer, passing his mother while she was in her daze. "Sara, is that really a ghost? I mean, Jacob, that's the name I heard you calling before. A real ghost, WOW! Wait'll..."

Sara walked over to where Eddie stood and grabbed him by the front of his shirt. She pulled him close to her face, glaring deeply into his eyes, "You are not to tell anyone about this! Do you understand, Eddie? NO ONE! Absolutely NO ONE!"

Eddie looked at Sara and realized that his sister meant business, "Yeah, yeah, no one. Sara, I won't tell anybody, I promise. WOW, a real ghost, WOW!"

"Eddie, I will make your life miserable for the rest of your life if you utter one word to anyone...even Dad!"

"I promise, Sara, I promise."

Sara eased her grip on Eddie's shirt and he relaxed into his previous posture, his eyes still round with wonder.

After Jean had regained her composure, Dr. Schiller moved back to where he was just an arm's length away from Jacob's ghost, "You needn't explain who or what you are young man. Sara told me all about you and I have already researched the raid, so I understand your predicament."

"Sir, if you don't mind my interrupting, but all I really want is to go home."

"And home is in Massachusetts?"

"Yes, sir, to be exact, Stow, Massachusetts."

"Indeed, which means we must move your gravesite, that is, your remains to a location in Stow, Massachusetts?"

"Yes sir."

"Hmmm, that could indeed prove problematic. Sara, you told me that you have inquired as to what is involved in moving his remains?"

"Yes, Dr. Schiller, and the easiest way is if Jacob has descendants in Stow and they request his reburial."

"And there are none?"

"Not that I could locate through the internet. Plus, any grave moving has to be approved through the Veterans Administration. Tyler found out…"

Jean suddenly came to life, "You mean Tyler knows about this?"

Sara nodded her head "Yes".

"And you couldn't even tell me about it?"

"Mom, you would have thought I was crazy. You already did anyway. And besides, I did tell you, remember?"

Jean opened her mouth to answer and then decided otherwise and closed her mouth, an apologetic look in her eyes.

"Sara," Dr. Schiller interrupted, "let me look into the VA requirements and we'll see if we can sidestep some of the issues ahead of us."

Sara turned to Jacob, "See, Jacob, I told you he would help us. Be patient, and I'll keep you posted as to the progress we make. If all goes well, we'll have you out of here and in Massachusetts before one bulldozer comes near here."

"Sara, what is a bull-dozer?" Jacob asked.

"I'll explain later when we've got more time." Sara looked at the others, "Are you ready to go?"

Eddie and Jean's eyes grew wide again and Sara turned just in time to watch Jacob's mist dissolve into the rock at the head of his grave.

"That's where he's buried. The third rock is his marker."

"You, you mean there's more?" Jean stammered.

"Yes, four, but only Jacob is here as a ghost. I guess the others moved on," Sara had turned to look at the stones and now turned back to look at her mother. Jean had her hands on her head seemingly to hold it on. Still pale, she was quavering a little bit. Dr. Schiller stepped over to Jean and sat her down and then put her head between her knees, "Sit there and keep your head between your knees until you feel better," he told the woman.

Sara and Eddie stood nearby and Sara could see the exhilaration in Eddie's expression. "Eddie, remember…"

"I know, Sara, not a word."

After a few minutes, Jean stood and the group returned to the house. As Dr. Schiller prepared to leave, Sara walked with him out to his car, "Sara, now that I've met Jacob, and know that he is not a figment of your imagination, we can start moving forward in getting your Jacob problem solved. Have you thought ahead as to how you are going to get his bones to Massachusetts? That's a long way."

"I haven't had a chance to think that far ahead, Dr. Schiller."

"Well, you leave it to me. I'll try and figure this all out for you."

"Thank you, Dr. Schiller."

Chapter Twenty One

After returning to the house, Jean walked upstairs and into Jack's study. As she entered, the steady click, click, click of the keyboard stopped. Jack turned to look at his wife, and then exclaimed, "Jean, what in the world…"

Jean stood looking at Jack as if she had seen another ghost. Her skin was pale and a fine sweat had broken out along her forehead. She stared straight ahead and was unable to speak. She was still not fully recovered from her experience in the woods.

"Honey, are you alright? Sit down before you fall down." Jack took hold of Jean's arms and moved her gently toward a chair. Once she sat down she looked up into Jack's eyes as she tried to speak, "Jack… Jack…" Jean let out a huge breath.

"Jean, you're scaring me. What in the world is going on? Are you feeling okay?"

Jean's field of vision had moved away from Jack's face and now she moved her head back to where she was staring into his eyes once again, "Jack… I have just seen the most, the most fantastic thing." Jean had exhausted herself with those few words.

"Jean, what are you talking about?"

"Sara's friend… I would have never guessed…," Jean grabbed Jack's shirt, "Jack, she's not crazy after all…,"

"Jean, you've got to make more sense. You're not making any sense. Saa-raa," Jack called out desperately.

Sara came running into the room and stopped abruptly when she saw her father kneeling on the floor in front of her mother who seemed to be babbling. Jack looked up imploringly at Sara, "What is wrong with your mother? She's not making any sense."

Sara looked at her Dad with a guilty expression, "I guess it's because of Jacob."

"Jacob? Who's Jacob?"

Jean suddenly snapped out of her stupor, "Sara's friend. Jacob is Sara's friend. Jack, Sara's friend is a ghost. Isn't that incredible?"

Jack was looking back and forth, from Jean to Sara and back again. It was like watching a ping pong game. Suddenly he stopped and yelled out, "Will somebody tell me what's going on?"

Jean fell silent and Sara seemed to snap to attention, "Dad, it's a very long story."

"We've got time." Jack said firmly.

About that time Eddie, having heard his father, came running into the room. He looked at all three parties involved in the conversation and soon realized what was being discussed.

Jack looked at Eddie, "Do you know what is going on?"

Eddie looked to Sara and then back to his Father and made the zipping motion across his lips.

"What is that supposed to mean?" Jack asked.

"I can't tell," was Eddie's reply.

Jack looked from one party to the next until out of pure frustration he announced, "Well someone is going to let me in on what's going on or we're going to be here all night." Looking from Eddie to Sara, Jack then said, "One of you is going to tell me what has got your mother so unnerved."

Sara let out a huge sigh and seemed to deflate. Turning to Eddie and knowing he would explode if he didn't tell, she said, "Go ahead, Eddie, Tell Dad. I'll let you off the hook."

Eddie's eyes got huge and he sucked in a huge breath and then the words came exploding out, "DAD! You are not going to believe this. We have a ghost, I mean Sara's got a ghost, well, that is, there is a ghost... a real live ghost, well I guess if he's a ghost he's not really alive..."

"Eddie, for crying out loud!" Sara yelled at her brother. Turning to her Dad, Sara continued the explanation, not leaving out any details, including her mother's introduction to Jacob,"... and Dad, that's why I've been moody. It's not the move down here. I'm not mad at you guys, it's just that I've made a promise to Jacob and I'm going to keep my promise. He is relying on me and I won't disappoint him."

Through the entire explanation Jean had slowly come back to the here and now and was listening to Sara's story. When Sara was finished explaining, Jean reached over and placed her hand on Sara's cheek, a sad smile on her face, "Sara, how can you ever forgive us for thinking you were… crazy. I don't even like saying the word. If only we'd known…"

"Mom, if I had told you the truth, would you really have believed me. I mean, really?"

Jean chuckled lightly, "I guess not, but boy, what a shock. I was not ready for that at all. You might have at least warned me."

"Really Mom, how would I have warned you, 'Oh, by the way, Mom, Dr. Schiller and I are going out to meet with my favorite neighborhood ghost; wanna come?' Really, mom, would you have believed me? You'd have thought both Dr. Schiller and I were crazy."

"I guess you're right, but, boy what a shock."

Jack was still kneeling on the floor in front of Jean and his expression was one of mixed emotions, "I don't know what to think. This all sounds so fantastic; so unbelievable. If you want to know the truth, it sounds like a novel or some cheap flick."

On his drive home from the encounter with Jacob, Dr. Schiller called Agatha, "Hello, Agatha, Dr. Schiller."

"Why hello Dr. Schiller, have you met your spiritual friend?"

"Yes, that is why I am calling. Agatha, my suspicions were correct. My patient has, indeed, met a ghost. He is a young Union soldier from the Civil War and his spirit is stuck here because he wants to go home. He was injured and died where his body lies in Ponce de Leon. My patient has promised to carry out the task, but because of her age, she is frustrated and angry because she doesn't know what to do."

"Dr. Schiller, you must help this young girl succeed in her mission. It is imperative that this young man's remains be returned to his home. He will wander aimlessly until someone performs this task. I am assuming that this patient of yours is a youngster?"

"Yes, she is fifteen, and I believe the two, ghost and mortal are developing an infatuation with each other which is also causing her some problems."

"That is quite normal, Dr. Schiller. The problems of those wanting to reach the other side can often evoke feelings of concern from those on our side and a girl that age, oh my, she is quite susceptible."

"Agatha, I am at a loss as to what to do for this poor girl and her friend."

"Dr. Schiller, you must do what you can to help them accomplish their mission. As absurd as it sounds, the peace of this poor boy's spirit is in your hands. It is your obligation to help them."

"I was afraid you were going to say that, Agatha. Is there any other way other than getting the boy's remains back to Massachusetts?"

"I am sorry, Dr. Schiller, but no. That is the poor boy's needs and until they are met, he will remain in this world."

"There is one other problem, Agatha. There will soon be construction in the area of his remains."

"Oh, my, that is serious. If his bones are disturbed other than according to his wishes, his spirit will remain here and at unrest for eternity. The boy will be lost to roam this plane of existence forever. Dr. Schiller, you must act quickly. His peace requires it."

Dr. Schiller gave out a frustrated sigh and then replied to Agatha, "I will take your suggestion under advisement, Agatha. Thank you so much for your help."

"Anytime I can help you Dr. Schiller, please feel free to call."

"Thank you, Agatha, until we meet again. Goodbye."

"Goodbye, Doctor."

The next day, on the drive to school, Sara was bursting with energy to tell Tyler about Dr. Schiller's visit, but before she could get started, they had arrived at the school parking lot and it was then that Sara found out that Courtney was back. She was sitting and waiting as Tyler and Sara pulled into the school parking lot. Sara spotted her right away and just by the expression on Courtney's face, Sara knew that her problems with Courtney were not over.

As soon as Tyler turned the motor off Sara was out the door and heading for the school building. She looked over at Tyler and said, "I'll catch you at lunch, Tyler. I have a lot to tell you, but now is not the time. Courtney's watching us and I don't want any more trouble. See ya later."

Sara had not told Tyler about Dr. Schiller's visit so she was anxious to talk to him at lunch. Throughout her morning classes, it was difficult for Sara to concentrate on her studies. Jacob and his problem kept interrupting her thoughts.

When lunch finally arrived, Sara made for her locker to drop off her books. She opened the locker door and placed her books on one of the shelves, but before she got too involved in getting things straightened out in her locker she heard footsteps approach behind the door. Before the door could bonk her in the head, Sara grabbed the door and slammed it shut, expecting to see Courtney standing there.

Instead, Tyler was standing there grinning at her. "Geez, Tyler, you scared the begeezes out of me. I thought you were Courtney."

Tyler laughed lightly, "Soorry, Sara, didn't mean to scare ya. Jus' thought I'd walk with ya to the cafeteria."

Once the two teens were at their usual table they went into a huddle to discuss Dr. Schiller. While they were talking they didn't notice one of Courtney's close friends, Adora Campbell, move to the table right next to them. Sara just kept her eyes on Courtney who was at her usual table some distance away.

Sara told Tyler everything that had gone on in the grove, "Tyler, that Dr. Schiller wasn't even surprised to see Jacob. My Mom, man, she went catatonic. And Eddie, I thought he was going to explode he was so excited."

"Did you get anything figured out?"

"Dr. Schiller said he would contact the VA and take care of that end," Sara grabbed Tyler's hand out of enthusiasm, "Tyler, I really think we are going to pull this off. But I think it's going to be up to us to transport the bones, or at least dig them up."

"Whatever it takes, I'm with ya, Sara." Tyler placed his hand over Sara's and beamed with affection.

Sara looked down at his hand and then looked up and over at Courtney. She could almost see steam pouring out of Courtney's ears, she looked that angry. She pulled her hand away from Tyler's and said, "I think we better leave. Courtney looks like she might explode."

"Forget Courtney, I have."

"The point is, Tyler, I don't think Courtney has forgotten you."

Tyler looked over at Courtney and frowned. Then the two, Tyler and Sara, stood and left the cafeteria together. Adora, in the meantime, had moved back over to the table and she and Courtney were now huddled together, talking.

"Adora, what did they say. I saw that Yankee witch holding Tyler's hand...what did they say?"

"I ain't 'xactly sure, Courtney. Theuh was somethin' 'bout a doctaw and a guy name of Jacob and somethin' 'bout diggin' up some bones."

At that last comment, Courtney reared back from her huddle with Adora and looked at her friend like she was nuts, "Bones? Diggin' up bones? Adora, are you shur?"

"I thin' that's wha' they said."

Courtney looked away and toward the door where Tyler and Sara had exited the cafeteria. Her eyes took on their angry squint and then she mumbled, "We'll just see about that. Bones, huh?" The last sound was a blast of air let out in contempt.

Adora just sat back silently, knowing when it was best to keep her comments to herself, especially around Courtney.

Chapter Twenty Two

Dr. Schiller got off the phone after a frustrating two hours trying to find someone who had the right answers. Eventually he had reached a man by the name of Bartholomew. He seemed another cog in that huge wheel called the Veterans Administration.

No one, not even Mr. Bartholomew, seemed to grasp the severity of the situation, but then Dr. Schiller couldn't be as forthcoming with information as he would have liked, especially when Mr. Bartholomew asked about Dr. Schiller's knowledge of the burial site and how he came to know that the person buried there was truly a Union Civil War soldier. Dr. Schiller knew from experience that the man would not believe how he knew about the validity of the grave's contents.

Mr. Bartholomew became quite indignant when Dr. Schiller couldn't or wouldn't answer his questions. Dr. Schiller had claimed doctor-patient privilege and that had rankled the man, but Mr. Bartholomew made it quite clear that there was a set procedure for this type of action after positive identification was made of the remains, and anything short of that proper procedure violated numerous laws.

Knowing the situation with Jacob's spirit and the immediacy brought about by the threat of bulldozers razing Jacob's burial site, Dr. Schiller decided that things would just have to be done their own way and the government be hanged. He didn't like doing things that way, especially if it was breaking the law, but sometimes, well… sometimes you just had to take those chances. Sometimes the workings of bureaucracy take far too long and Dr. Schiller felt like this was one of those times. So he decided to start putting together a plan.

Dr. Schiller's attitude harkened back to his college days when as a student activist he helped lead several protests against government programs, and hearing of Jacob's problem it revived those rebellious feelings.

Later he called Jean Richardson, Sara's mother, and told her of what he had found out. "What have you got planned, doctor?" Jean asked.

"What we will have to do, and in order to protect Jacob's spirit I truly feel that we have no choice, is that, with your permission, I will escort the two kids to Massachusetts. After they have dug up Jacob's bones, we will fly up and see to their burial."

"But Dr. Schiller, we can't afford plane fare for even Sara, let alone Tyler. We live on a very tight budget."

"I understand, Mrs. Richardson, but I will pay for the tickets. It will be tax deductible as part of my treatment plan; after all, Sara is my patient."

Jean smiled to herself as she thought, *devious, Dr. Schiller, very devious.*

Jean and Dr. Schiller set about devising the plan for the removal and reburial of the remains of Jacob Wilcott.

When Sara arrived home from school that day, Jean called her into the kitchen. Sitting at the table, she explained the details of what Dr. Schiller had told her.

Sara sat back wide eyed at her mother's complicity in the plan, "Mom, you're going along with this? I can't believe that you would go along with something like this, especially breaking the law. What will Dad think? What about Eddie?"

"Before I discuss anything else, Sara, I want to ask, why are you so intent on getting Jacob home?"

Sara sat thinking about her mother's question while Jean watched the changes on Sara's face as the girl went mentally through her reasons. Then Sara looked at her mother, "Mom, I love Jacob. I want to help him and this is the only way I can do that."

Jean looked at Sara, "Really? Sara, you're only fifteen, what do you know of love?"

"Mom, love doesn't have an age limit attached to it. Kids can love. Eddie and I love you and Dad."

"That's a different kind of love, Sara."

"Maybe, but love none the less, besides who says that I

am too young to know how to love someone my own age?'"

"Sara, this boy isn't even alive. He's a ghost. He died over a hundred years ago."

"Exactly, Mom, and what chance has he ever got to love someone else. I feel things in here for Jacob," Sara put her hand to her chest, "that I have never felt for anyone else and Jacob loves me. I can't tell you exactly why I want to do this for him other than I just know that I must. I have promised him and I'm going to do exactly what I promised. I am not going to break my promise to him. He is depending on me." By now Sara was in tears, her heart breaking for Jacob. "Mom, why are you doing this? Why can't you just accept what I need to do?"

"Sara, this is a major responsibility and, a huge undertaking. This isn't just a drive up the road. But…I think I understand where you're coming from, I had a boyfriend when I was your age and I would have moved heaven and earth for him. Sara, I'm not telling you no. I just want you to understand the why's. I want you to be sure of the reasons. Besides, you forget, Sara, I saw Jacob, too. And despite my shock, I felt sorry for that young man, uh, ghost, and his predicament. My heart went out to him. Plus, Sara, I want to help you. I love you, sweetie, and I don't like to see you so disturbed. Besides, Dr. Schiller has taken on all responsibility for his actions if anyone asks.

"Don't get me wrong, Sara, this is a very difficult decision for me to make, and it really doesn't make sense. People are going to think me crazy and irresponsible, but I also realize how important this is to you and I want you to be well."

Jean reached out and took Sara's hand, "Listen, Sara, I am willing to do whatever it takes to help you… and Jacob, of course. So if Dr. Schiller thinks that he can pull this off then I will do what I can. You and Tyler will be acting on your own. If anyone asks, your father and I, even Eddie, won't have any knowledge of what is going on. Do you get my meaning?"

Sara nodded her head as tears filled her eyes and blurred her vision, "Thanks, Mom." Sara paused to take a deep breath, "You know, Mom, every time I think that the gap between us is growing wider I realize I'm wrong. Every time I think you don't care about me, or my feelings, you do something to prove me wrong." Sara smiled at her mother as a few remaining tears trickled down her cheeks.

"It takes a brave person to say that, Sara. From this point forward, if you are going to accomplish this for Jacob, you are going to need to be very brave, and strong." Jean squeezed Sara's hand, "and… on your best behavior. Do you understand?"

Sara gave her mother a knowing smile, "I understand, Mom. Best behavior, cross my heart."

Sara suddenly widened her eyes, "Mom, what about Dad and Eddie? I mean, how do we keep them out of the loop?"

"You let me handle that end. Dr. Schiller will take care of the travel plans. I will take care of the home front, and you and Tyler will take care of procuring Jacob's bones and transporting them to the final destination."

"When are we going to do this?"

"I'm not sure. Dr. Schiller will get back to us when he has made the reservations."

Sara tried to call Tyler to tell him of the developments, but he wasn't home so she decided to tell him the next day at school. Instead she headed for the woods to tell Jacob.

Once she was in the clearing she called out to Jacob. He appeared immediately just above his marker stone. She sat down at her tree and Jacob came to sit beside her, "Are things well with you, Sara? I notice a bit of apprehension on your part." Jacob reached out and took Sara's hands in his. To Sara it felt as if a kitten had curled around her hands. The feeling was soft and warm. Sara felt a tenderness she had never experienced before.

Sara turned toward Jacob and her words, edgy with excitement, tumbled out, "Jacob, it's almost… I mean, it's going to happen. Oh, Jacob, we are going to make it happen. Dr. Schiller is making the arrangements now and soon, we'll have you… home." Sara's words came slower and softer until her last words were mere whispers as she realized that once they had Jacob's remains moved, he would no longer be here.

"Oh, Jacob, what am I going to do? If we get your bones moved you'll no longer be here. I won't be able to see you or talk to you," Sara paused as the realization came crashing down. "Oh, Jacob, I want to help you, but I don't want to lose you."

Once again the tears began to flood Sara's eyes, "Oh, why do I always cry?" she hung her head in shame and disgust at her inability to control her emotions.

Sara felt a soft and tender trace along her cheek. She looked up into Jacob's face, now only inches from hers, and despite his solemn expression, Sara saw nothing but love in his eyes.

Sara closed her eyes as Jacob kissed her lips softly and tenderly. What she felt she could only imagine because other than a soft whisper of air upon her lips Sara could feel nothing but the love in her heart.

Sara opened her eyes to see Jacob pull back slightly, "I will miss you, Sara, and I will never forget what you are doing for me, but I really must go home. I think I am falling in love with you, Sara, but I realize that we could never have a true life together. I am only a specter of what I once was. You understand, don't you Sara?"

Sara sat up, straightening her back as she wiped the tears away from her cheeks and chin. She sniffed her nose and looked at Jacob, "I know, Jacob, I know… I love you, too and I will see that you get home just like I promised." Sara's resolve was set in stone. If asked why, she could not have given an answer, but to Sara, this was a promise she was going to keep. Her feelings for Jacob were unexplainable and yet, they were there, deep within her heart.

Chapter Twenty Three

The next day on the drive to school Sara tried to explain to Tyler all that had taken place, but she didn't want to get into a long explanation that she wouldn't be able to finish on the short drive. So instead she said, "I'll explain everything at lunch. It's long and involved and I want enough time to explain it all."

Tyler was good with that so the two teens vowed to meet at lunch to discuss the 'Jacob situation'. When they arrived at the school Sara kept her eyes busy looking for Courtney. As they pulled in to park, Sara spotted Courtney in her usual place off to one side sitting with her friends on some steps into the school. Courtney's eyes were little angry slits as they followed Tyler's truck until it stopped. Then Courtney's eyes followed Sara as she left Tyler and entered the school. Sara just considered things were not going to change so she prepared herself for the day and waited until lunch.

Later, Sara looked through the door as she entered the cafeteria. She spotted Tyler sitting at their usual table. Just beyond, Sara could see Courtney seated in her usual location with some of her friends filling the other seats at her table, the worker bees seemingly gathered around the queen bee.

What Sara didn't see was who was sitting just behind Tyler. Located at the table next to Sara and Tyler's regular spot, their backs to Tyler, was Adora and her boyfriend, easily within earshot of where Sara and Tyler would be talking.

Sara walked over and sat across from Tyler. She looked beyond him and saw Courtney glaring at her with her usual angry eyes. Sara looked at Tyler, "I thought you were going to tell Courtney you weren't interested in her?"

"Naw, I figured if I just ignored her, she'd jus' finally give up, but she's like a tick; she grabs holda' somethin' an' won't give up."

Sara chuckled at Tyler's analogy. While they ate, Sara began her tale, not leaving out any details including her mother's reaction, "Dr. Schiller acted like seeing a ghost was something he was used to. He didn't seem surprised at all. Later, he called my Mom and told her that he tried to get some information from the VA about moving a Civil War grave and couldn't get anywhere, just some run around about breaking laws. The guy that Dr. Schiller talked to said that without a positive identification of the bones, well, nothing could be done, legally.

"So here's the deal; Dr. Schiller is going to buy the plane tickets to Massachusetts. He'll let us know when he has them and then we have to dig up the bones and meet him at the airport. We'll fly to Massachusetts and then go to the cemetery where we will rebury the bones. He also said that let the VA and the laws be hanged. He was going to do this anyway."

Tyler leaned in closer to ask, "What about your Mom and Dad?"

"Mom said if anyone asks, they'll just dummy up; they won't know a thing. After the bones are buried, we fly home. Jacob's home, we're home and no one's the wiser. Those bulldozers can wreak havoc on the countryside all they want."

Tyler's eyes had almost glazed over with excitement, "Geez, Sara, I never been away from home bafor! Not like this. This is goin' ta be excitin'."

"Sad too, I'm going to miss Jacob. But this is what he wants so this is what he's going to get."

Sara looked up at the clock on the wall, "I gotta go to my locker before the bell. Wanna walk with me?"

"Shore, let's go," Tyler replied. Tyler and Sara got up and left the cafeteria.

As soon as they had departed, Adora got up from her reconnaissance position and returned to Courtney's table. As she sat, Courtney cleared the table of all her other friends, "Okay, everybody, clear out. I gotta talk to Adora."

The other girls grudgingly stood and took the remainder of their lunches to another table in the cafeteria as Courtney and Adora put their heads together, "Well, what did they say, Adora?"

"More jus like thu othur day, Courtney. They talked about diggin' up bones and flyin' them to Massachustts."

"**MASSACHUSETTS?**" Courtney practically yelled it out. "Adora, are you sure?"

"I'm positive, Courtney; they said Massachusetts. An' they said they was gonna fly with some doctaw an' then they was gonna rebury the bones up thereh.

"They talked about the bones bein' from some Civil War Union soldier an' they said, the doctaw said the laws be hanged, so it sounds like they're gonna break the law."

"Ya think?" Courtney answered sarcastically. She didn't understand what Sara and Tyler were plotting, but if it was breaking the law then she saw her chance to get back at that Yankee witch for stealing Tyler away from her. "Well, we'll just see about that!"

Courtney grabbed Adora's hand, "Adora, don't say a word about this to anybody until I have a chance to talk to my Daddy. He'll know how to handle this."

That evening when Courtney's father came home from work he was met at the door by his daughter. Courtney's expression was beyond forlorn as she asked her daddy for a moment of his time.

"What has got my little princess all upset? You haven't been picked on at school again by that girl, have you?"

"No, Daddy, but it does have something to do with her." Courtney began to wring her hands and allowed her eyes to tear slightly, "Daddy, ya know I really like Tyler Infinger?"

"So's ya said, Honey. Now, what's this all about?"

"Well, Daddy, this Yankee girl has got him all tied up in some kind of law breaking. He's gonna get hisself into some really hot water and end up in prison." By now Courtney was crying and had her Daddy entirely twined around her little finger.

"Now, now, Baby, ya know I've never denied ya anythin'. What can I do ta hep ya?"

"I don't know, Daddy. It seems this girl has got Tyler wrapped up with somethin' to do with moving some Civil War grave an' they're gonna take the bones to Massachusetts of all places." By now Courtney's voice had reached a wail as she continued her tale to her father, "Oh, Daddy, I don't want to see Tyler end up in jail." Courtney ended her statement with huge crocodile tears and a blubbering that would rival the most tragic scene in 'Gone with the Wind'.

Courtney's father pulled her to him and hugged her tightly, "Now don't you fret, Darlin'. I know jus who to talk to, so I'll take care of this. I'll make sure nothin' happens to Tyler, okay?"

Courtney nodded her head in compliance as she sniffled and wiped the forced tears from her cheeks. She turned from her father and left the room, a satisfied expression on her face and a vengeful look in her eyes.

The next day, from his office at the Ponce de Leon City Hall Jessie Alford, Courtney's father, placed a call to an old college friend at the Veterans Administration, "Joseph, this is Jessie...Alford."

"Jessie, how ya doin' boy?"

"Good, good. Haven't seen ya for a while."

"Not since the last alumni rally; 'Go Gators!'

Joseph Bartholomew chuckled lightly and then asked, "What can I do for ya, Jessie?"

"Listen here, Joseph, I got a problem with a couple a kids that go to my daughter's high school. Seems they've found a Civil War grave and intend on moving it somewhere's up north."

"You're the second person I've spoken to recently about a similar situation only I didn't know exactly where it was. Some doctor called me about it. I took notes somewhere." Joseph Bartholomew scrambled through the papers on his desk.

"Now we can't have every Tom, Dick or Harry digging up bones any old time they feel like it. That just won't do. There are proper procedures for this sort of thing. What would it be like if people just started digging up bones any old time they felt like it. No, no this won't do. That's why we have laws!"

Jessie could hear the sound of papers being shuffled

around and drawers being slid open and closed as Joseph searched for his notes. Suddenly a loud voice echoed through his phone, "Found it, hot dawg, I found it; man's name is Schiller, Dr. Schiller. You know the man?"

"No, can't say that I do, but I'll certainly find out and get back to ya soon. Nice talkin' to ya, Joseph."

"You too, Jessie. Get back to me on this A.S.A.P. will ya. We can't have people breakin' the law. We gotta move on this before they disturb even one bone."

"I'll call you as soon as I hear anything else. Mind if I call you at home cuz it might be this evening before I find out anymore."

"No problem, Jessie, call me when you get any more information."

"Will do, Joseph…Go Gators!"

The two men hung up the phone, both of them chuckling.

Chapter Twenty Four

The imposing man walked through the office door. He flashed his ID at the receptionist and spoke in a loud and authoritative voice, "My name is Bartholomew and I need to speak with Dr. Schiller."

The receptionist looked back at the man, her eyes wide with astonishment. She blinked her eyes a few times and then asked, "Is the doctor expecting you, he's currently with a patient?"

"No, he's not expecting me. He called me recently and I am returning his inquiry."

The receptionist stood, seemingly a bit flustered, "Please have a seat, sir. I'll let the doctor know you are here. Your name is?"

"Bartholomew," the man answered curtly.

A few minutes after the receptionist disappeared through a door, Dr. Schiller stepped into his waiting room and addressed the waiting man, "Mr. Bartholomew, how nice of you to visit me at my office. What can I help you with?" Dr. Schiller was not happy to see Mr. Bartholomew in his office, but he was not the kind of person to be rude and just ask the man to leave. Instead he stated, "I have a patient right now, if you don't mind waiting, I will be finished in about thirty minutes."

"Fine, I'll read a magazine." Mr. Bartholomew snatched up a magazine off a near-by table and started ruffling through the pages. Dr. Schiller retreated back through the door and disappeared from sight.

Some minutes later the receptionist spoke loudly, "Mr. Bartholomew, Dr. Schiller can see you now."

Mr. Bartholomew slammed the magazine down on the table and stood formidably, straightening his jacket and vest before stepping toward the door.

As Mr. Bartholomew stepped into Dr. Schiller's office, the doctor followed on his heels, motioning Mr. Bartholomew to a large chair. After Mr. Bartholomew was seated, Dr. Schiller then sat at his desk. Looking directly at the man from the Veterans Administration, Dr. Schiller spoke, "Mr. Bartholomew, to what can I attribute this unexpected visit?"

"Dr. Schiller, you are the one who called me."

"True, but I thought our conversation had been resolved when I hung up the phone."

"Well, I did answer your questions, but I have received some additional information and now I am asking the questions."

Dr. Schiller's eyebrows shot up, "Excuse me?"

"Dr. Schiller, it has come to my attention that there are a couple of teenagers in the Ponce de Leon area that are going to attempt to move a Civil War grave. Do you have any knowledge of this?"

"None whatsoever Mr. Bartholomew, and as I said before, by law, I can not disclose to you or any other authority any information disclosed to me by a patient. Do you understand that?"

Mr. Bartholomew sat back as if Dr. Schiller had hit him. He blinked his eyes a couple of times and then seemed to change his attitude. "I apologize, Dr. Schiller, but I feel very strongly about this. It is the responsibility of the Veterans Administration, and I feel very strongly about this, to keep safe all those gravesites of our veterans from unnecessary disturbance, be they two years old, or two hundred. The resting places of our confederate or union forces are as sacrosanct as those of our newly fallen and I feel compelled to step in whenever I feel that a great wrong will be done to one of our fallen veterans."

"Mr. Bartholomew, I merely inquired as to the protocol of doing this. I did not intimate that there was an actual removal about to take place and because this has to do with a patient, I cannot divulge any further information. I cannot give you any locations or names of those inquiring. I'm sorry, but your trip here, today, was useless. You will leave here today with no more information than when you arrived. Now, if you don't mind, I have patients to see."

Mr. Bartholomew stood, less than satisfied, and turned to leave. Pausing at the door, he looked at Dr. Schiller, "Thank you for your time, doctor, but be assured… this is not over with. I will be watching. I work for the government… and we have eyes and ears everywhere, Dr. Schiller!"

Dr. Schiller raised his hands in an 'oh well' gesture and tipped his head slightly sideways, meaning just that.

Later that afternoon, Dr. Schiller called Jean Richardson, "Hello, Mrs. Richardson, this is Dr. Schiller."

"Yes, Dr. Schiller, what can I do for you?"

"I had an unexpected visitor today."

There was silence at the other end of the phone.

"Mr. Bartholomew from the Veterans Administration here in Panama City came to my office."

"Why?"

"Someone from up there knows about Jacob and the moving of his grave. That is what it seemed to me from what Bartholomew said."

"But who?"

"What about the girl that Sara had the fight with?"

"Courtney? But how could she?"

"Perhaps she overheard Sara and Tyler talking at school."

"I'll ask Sara when she gets home."

"Please keep me apprised of any new information, Mrs. Richardson."

"I will, Dr. Schiller, I will, and thank you for calling."

"Good day, Mrs. Richardson."

"Good bye Dr. Schiller."

That afternoon when Sara arrived home from school, Jean was waiting with questions. "Sara, does Courtney know anything about what you or Tyler are doing?"

Sara's eyes bugged slightly, "Courtney? Heck no, Mom. We don't tell her anything."

"Could she have overheard you and Tyler talking?"

"Golly, not that I know of. We only talk in the cafeteria and I have my eyes on Courtney the whole time. She sits at another table across the cafeteria from us."

"Well, someone knows and they have alerted a man at the VA. The man came to see Dr. Schiller today and the man warned him about having anything to do with moving a Civil War grave."

Sara's eyes bugged out even more, "But how could he know?"

"Dr. Schiller thought it might have been Courtney."

"Geez, Mom, I'll talk to Tyler and I'll keep a close eye on everyone who sits near us. Maybe Courtney's had someone listening in while Tyler and I talk."

"Maybe you'd better not talk about it at school."

"Yeah, maybe you're right."

The next day Sara told Tyler about what was going on while they drove to school. "Great, that's just what we need, the dang law gittin' in on this deal."

"Well, let's just be very observant at lunch and see who sits at the tables around us. It could be that Courtney's got extra ears out there, know what I mean?"

"Yeah, I know what ya mean. I wish I'd neveh met that gurl."

Courtney was watching when they arrived at the school and when Sara and Tyler left the truck and walked toward the school Tyler shot Courtney the nastiest look he could come up with. Courtney looked like someone had slapped her. She literally rocked back and got a shocked look to her eyes.

Sara looked at Tyler with a smile, "I think she got your message that time."

"I hope so!"

While Sara and Tyler were at school Jean received another call from Dr. Schiller, "Jean, Dr. Schiller here. I've got the tickets; we fly out on Saturday morning so tell Sara and Tyler to get Jacob ready to go by Friday afternoon and meet me at the Panama City Airport no later than eight am Saturday morning. We will fly out almost immediately and return Sunday evening."

"Oh, Dr. Schiller, is everything going to be alright. I mean, what about that VA guy?"

"I think I've got everything figured out, even if there is a problem. Just tell the kids to bring a small carryon with a change of clothes and we'll get Operation "Yankee Boy" completed."

"But Doctor Schiller, what about the laws?"

"Look, Jean, I am not new to the spirit world. That is why I wanted to see Sara's 'friend'. And from my experience a spirit caught in this world will be stuck here until their needs are met. And once that happens, their spirit is released to go where it needs to.

"This boy's spirit is destined to stay right here until his needs are met and those needs are that his bones be buried in his home town. So I find it my responsibility to help Jacob's spirit be set to rest and that means moving his bones to Stow, Massachusetts. And if the government won't help...then the laws be hanged. It is my moral and ethical responsibility."

With a worried expression, Jean said, "Okay Dr. Schiller, I'll make sure the kids are there. Oh, doctor, what airline will they find you at?"

"Boy, I'm sure glad you thought to ask. Delta, we'll be

flying Delta. Tell them to look for me at the Delta ticket counter."

"Will do; onward and upward with Operation "Yankee Boy". Oh, Doctor, one more question. What about the bones. I mean, how are you going to get them through the x-rays at security?"

"I'm glad you asked. I have a label to put on the package carrying the bones that is addressed to a forensic archeologist friend of mine in Boston and I will declare the package contents as we check it through so there will be no questions. They're just bones being personally delivered for identification and dating. With my credentials, no one will question. But please remember, you know nothing of my plans, correct?"

Jean smiled silently as she listened to Dr. Schiller's explanation, "Correct. You have thought and taken care of everything haven't you, Doctor?"

"I've tried, Mrs. Richardson."

"Oh, Dr. Schiller, please take care of my baby. She's very vulnerable right now. And I have never allowed her out on her own or in the hands of any other adults."

"I understand, Jean, I really do. Not only is it my business, but I have children of my own. I will watch out for both of them personally, barring any unforeseen circumstances. And I will return them home to you in just a few days."

"Thank you, Dr. Schiller, I'm sure you will take good care

of them."

When Sara walked into the cafeteria to meet Tyler she paid close attention to who was sitting near their regular table. She noticed Courtney looking at a blond sitting at another table just behind Tyler. Sara walked to one side of the room, looking at the girl whose back was facing Tyler.

When she got around far enough she was thunderstruck. She recognized the girl as one of those who had always been standing front and center in the group offering support when Courtney had attacked her. She wasn't sure of the girl's name but she knew she was definitely connected to Courtney.

Sara walked quickly to where Tyler was sitting and leaned close and said, "I've spotted our leak. Let's sit at another table. The two conspirators got up and moved to a table on the opposite side of the cafeteria, far away from listening ears.

Courtney followed their movements and when Sara once again made eye contact with Courtney she could see the girl's eyes had narrowed into her recognizable hate expression. "I think we just countered Courtney's intentions. Now we can talk."

"What have you heard from Dr. Schiller?" Tyler asked.

"Nothing yet, but I think we need to be prepared to move quickly. Have you said anything to your folks?"

"Nah, not yet. I don' think I'm gonna say exactly what we're doing. I think I'm jus' gonna tell um I'm gonna spend the night with a frien'. That they'll unnerstand and not question."

Sara took an excited deep breath, "I guess we'd better get out and dig up Jacob's bones."

"Yeah, let's do it after school today. I'll jus stay when I drop you off."

"Perfect. I know Jacob won't mind."

Later that afternoon after stopping the truck Tyler and Sara walked out toward the woods taking a shovel and a large cardboard box with them. Once they made it into the clearing Sara called for Jacob.

Jacob appeared almost immediately, "Hello Sara, you called me?"

Excitedly Sara smiled at him, "Jacob, we've come to collect your bones. Are you ready to go home?"

"Sara, I've been ready to go home for almost a hunnert un fifty years."

"Well, it's about to happen. We're getting packed up and ready to fly to Massachusetts."

"What do I need to do?"

"Nothing. Tyler and I are going to dig up your bones and put them in this box and take them back to my house, then we wait for Dr. Schiller to call. Once he calls it's off we go. You won't mind if we dig up your bones?"

"Not if it means I'm going home. By all means, dig." Jacob moved from his gravesite and drifted over to where Sara stood. Leaning closely to her he whispered, "Sara, I will never forget you or what you are doing for me."

Sara smiled softly as she heard his words, and then replied, "I'm happy I can help you, Jacob. I will be sorry when you are gone. But you won't be gone from my heart."

"Sara, you will never be gone from my heart no matter where my bones lie. And all you need to do is call me and I will hear you. I will be near."

"Thank you, Jacob."

Tyler looked at Sara with a disapproving expression tinged with a slight amount of jealousy, "We need to get started, Sara."

"Yes...yes...I know. Jacob, where do we start digging?"

Jacob moved over beyond the moss covered stone and pointed down. Tyler moved to the spot and jabbed the shovel into the soil. Removing several shovels full of soil he pushed the spade into the dirt once more only this time his effort was met with resistance as if he had hit a root.

"Sara, I think I've hit something. Could be a stone or..."

"Here, let me dig a little with my hands." Sara kneeled down and began working the soil with her fingers, sifting the fine, sandy soil through her hands. She wiggled her fingers down to break up the soil and felt something cylindrical, almost like a root. Grasping it with her fingers she pulled, meeting only a slight resistance. As she pulled, the stick gave way and Sara pulled up a long dirty white stick, or at least it looked like a stick. She lifted it slightly to get a better look and then turned it around to get a better idea of its shape. "Tyler, I think we have hit pay dirt, that is, Jacob. I think this is part of the arm. You know that one slim bone in the forearm."

Tyler looked off into the air for a few seconds, "I think it's called the… uh…"

"ULNA!" Sara hollered out.

"Yeah, that's the one." Tyler answered.

"We've found him," Sara gasped. "We've found him," she said in a much more subdued voice. Sara dropped her head as a trail of tears began to descend her cheek.

"What're yah cryin' for, Sara?" Tyler looked at his companion with concern.

"This makes it all real. I mean, this proves he was a real person…" Sara sat back on her behind and let out a small sob "…he really lived." Sara looked up where she saw Jacob's ghost leaning against a tree holding his left arm with his right as if he were hurt. "Oh… Jacob… does this hurt you?"

"No, Sara, not at all, but that is my arm bone you hold. And yes, I was real once, I truly lived."

"I am so sorry we have to do this, Jacob."

Jacob stepped forward and took Sara's chin in his hand. Sara felt a soft and tender lift to her chin and then she heard Jacob whisper, sounding almost as a sigh, "Sara, remember, you are helping me. Do what you must do. I do not mind."

"Come on, Sara, we gotta get this done." Tyler intruded into their intimate interlude.

Jacob leaned down and kissed Sara lightly on her cheek and Tyler rolled his eyes. Sara touched her cheek where she had felt the brief brush of air and smiled.

"Sara, come on, we gotta get this done." Tyler was beginning to get annoyed.

"I know Tyler, I know." Sara started moving the earth again with her hands and came up with another long bone placing it in the box where she had placed the first one. "Tyler, come on and help me dig with our hands. I don't want to break up his bones." Tyler looked a little disgusted at the prospect of handling the bones with his hands, but helped anyway.

It took the two teens better than an hour to scrape the dirt from the skeleton where it lay in the ground. Before removing anymore bones they removed the soil until finally they had the entire skeleton uncovered and laying bare, the bones naked and clean.

As they worked the soil they uncovered some buttons, a belt buckle and some leather remnants from his belt. Then inside the cavity formed by the rib bones, Sara found what looked like a small pebble. She worked the soil from it and then realized that it wasn't stone, but metal. Holding it up she said, "Tyler, what is this?"

Tyler took the small particle in his fingers and rolled it around realizing that it wasn't entirely round, but rather misshapen by impact. "Sara, this is the slug that killed Jacob. I've taken too many from deer that I've hunted. I know a spent slug."

Sara fell back landing on her backside once again as if she had been pushed. Her face turned ashen gray and her eyes teared up again.

"Come on, Sara, we gotta get goin' on this. It'll be dark before long and I don't want to be out here after dark." Tyler tried to prod Sara into action, "Look, we knew he had died from a gunshot wound."

"I know, but I didn't think we would find the bullet."

"Well, it was buried with him, and metal doesn't dissolve like wood or paper, so it's there where it was buried."

"I know, Tyler, I'm sorry." Sara sniffed away the tears and began working at the dirt, extracting the bones. When Sara reached the skull she reared back as the dirt filled orbs stared back at her. She reached out and gently ran her fingers over the cheek bones and around the openings where once Jacob's eyes had been. She paused long enough to look up at Jacob as he smiled lightly at her. "The things your eyes must have seen. Things I will never see." Sara said just above a whisper.

"Yes, that is true. I have seen many things in my short

life. But my most treasured visions are of you, Sara." Sara smiled wistfully at the specter standing mere feet from her.

By dusk the two, Sara and Tyler, had all of Jacob's bones in the box and were making their way back to the house.

Finally back in the kitchen with the box on the kitchen table, Tyler looked at Sara, "We've got to have something else to carry the bones in than jus' a cardboard box, Sara. You got any ideas?"

Sara thought about it for a moment, "How about a backpack. We can use mine from school." Sara ran into the other room and retrieved the pack, leaving a trail of school books and paper on tables and furniture as she moved back toward the kitchen. "Will this work?"

Tyler laid the longest bone up to the pack and then smiled at her, "Jus' right. Help me move the bones over."

The two teens worked quickly transferring the bones from the box to the pack and once every last small bone had been moved, Sara zipped up the bag. "Well, we're ready. Now, all we have to do is wait for Dr. Schiller."

Jean walked into the kitchen just then and heard Sara's last statement, "He's already called. You two are to meet him at the "Beaches Airport" tomorrow morning at eight in the morning. You will fly out almost immediately. He will meet you at the Delta desk."

Jean noticed movement out the corner of her eye and

looked over to see Jacob leaning against the kitchen door, "Why, hello Jacob. I'm surprised to see you here in the house."

Jacob nodded his head at Jean and then Sara said, "Mom, we have Jacob's bones here in the backpack. I guess where his bones are he is too."

"Welcome to my home, Jacob." Jean spread her arm in a welcoming manner.

Jacob nodded his head once again,"Thank you, ma'am."

A noise at the door drew everyone's attention away from Jacob and toward the door to the dining room. There stood Jack staring intently at Jacob. Jacob, realizing that this was a newcomer dissolved into mist that then disappeared into the backpack.

Sara, Tyler and Jean all watched as Jack turned a light shade of gray and then stammered, "Wha...wha...wha..."

Jean jumped up from her chair where she had been seated at the table and rushed over to Jack, "Jack, honey, Jack, it's okay, Jack, that's just Jacob."

Jack backed out of the doorway and Jean gently directed him to a chair. When his legs bumped into the chair he sat or actually collapsed into the seat, his arm raised and pointing at where Jacob had been standing. Now he was not uttering a sound but merely staring.

Jean looked around to Sara with a pleading expression and Sara rushed up to her father, "Dad, it's okay, That's Jacob, you know, the ghost we were telling you about." Sara looked up at her mom, "Mom, why doesn't he talk?" Turning back to her father, Sara spoke, "Dad, come on, Dad, wake up!" Sara looked at her mother, "Mom, we need to startle him,"

"How?" Jean looked at Sara, a panicked expression on her face.

Sara reached out and smacked her dad on the face. When that had no effect she did it again only harder, "Dad! Wake up!"

Jack blinked his eyes, but was still staring at where he had seen Jacob disappear. "Dad, for crying out loud, wake up, you're scaring us."

Sara went to slap him again, but Jack reached up and stopped her arm in motion, "I'm awake, kitten. I'm awake. What did I just see?"

Sara looked at her mother and then said, "You saw Jacob, my friend."

"Friend... what friend just turns into mist? What did I just see?"

"Dad, you saw Jacob, my friend. Remember when Mom saw him, we explained it to you? He's a ghost."

"But why is he here...in the house? I thought he was out in the woods."

"Well...he was until we brought his bones in here."

Jack looked around, his eyes quickly surveying the kitchen and dining room, "Bones...in here...in the house?"

Sara looked sheepishly at her mother and then looked at her father, "Yes, Dad, here in the house, in my backpack."

Jack looked at Sara and muttered in a whimpering manner, "Why?"

Sara looked at her mother with a pleading look, she wanted to explain everything to her Dad, but Jean moved her head in a side to side motion, warning Sara not to divulge the reason for bringing Jacob's bones into their kitchen.

Instead, Jean looked at Jack directly in his eyes, "Jack, why don't we go upstairs, you need to lay down. You've had quite a shock."

"Yeah, yeah...shock...lay down...good idea."

Sara and Jean helped Jack stand up and then directed his movement toward the staircase. Once at the staircase, Sara let go of her father's arm as Jean took him up to their room. Sara turned back to the kitchen where Tyler had been left.

As Sara entered the kitchen Tyler stood with an astonished expression and moved toward the back door, "Guess I better be goin'. I'll be back at about seven to pick ya up, Sara, and we'll head for the airport."

Sara smiled, "Tyler, I can't wait. This is going to be so exciting. I've never taken a plane flight."

"Me neithuh. I gotta pack and tell my folks I'll see'um on Sunday. Hope yo'r Dad'll be okay?"

Sara smiled and looked toward the ceiling, "He'll be okay. Mom will take care of him."

Tyler headed out the door, "See you in the morning, Sara. Be sure and bring yo'r backpack."

"Goodnight Tyler. See you in the morning."

Chapter Twenty Five

Tyler pulled into the Richardson's driveway exactly at seven the next morning. What Tyler didn't see was the car that pulled off the road blocking the driveway just after he pulled next to Sara's house.

Sara came running out of the house, a firm grip on her backpack, and climbed into Tyler's truck. Tyler backed slightly and then cut a circle and headed for the road. As they approached they saw the car and someone standing in the drive next to the car. Tyler stopped his truck.

Both Tyler and Sara were dumbstruck. The figure now standing in front of their truck was Courtney. Sara looked at Tyler, "I'll take care of this."

Sara climbed out of the truck and walked up defiantly to her nemesis, "Courtney, what are you doing here?"

"I'm making sure you don't get Tyler into any trouble."

"Trouble? You want trouble, do you? Well, I'm the one to give you trouble," Before Sara could take her threat any farther Jacob appeared by her side.

Courtney looked wide eyed at Jacob, "Who is he?"

"My friend and Tyler's."

"Everything alright, Sara?" Jacob asked.

"Yes, Jacob, thank you. Everything is just fine." Sara knew what would happen next.

Jacob dissolved into a mist and disappeared into the truck. Courtney stepped back stuttering and stammering. Then she turned white, her eyes rolled back into her head and she melted to the ground.

Sara turned to smile at Tyler and then signaled him to come help her. While Sara pulled Courtney out of the driveway Tyler pulled her car onto the shoulder and away from the driveway. When that was done he walked over to Sara, "You jus' gonna leave her here?"

Sara gave Tyler a sly smile and said, "No, let's put her in her car." The two teens picked the girl up, Sara grabbed her arms and Tyler, her legs and they carrrieded her over and sat her in the driver's seat, making it look like she had passed out at the wheel, "Let her explain that!" Then they ran back to the truck and headed to the airport, already running behind schedule.

Already at the airport terminal, Dr. Schiller moved through the lobby toward the Delta Desk. As he approached he noticed a familiar looking figure standing to one side. Realizing who the figure was, Dr. Schiller determined that Mr. Bartholomew had been following him, intent on spoiling his plans. Thinking quickly, Dr. Schiller started formulating a new plan.

Pulling into the airport, the two kids parked in a long term space, grabbed their duffel bags, the backpack and headed for the terminal. Once inside they looked for signs directing them to the Delta desk. As they moved quickly through the terminal lobby, following the signs they noticed ahead, already standing at the counter was Dr. Schiller. Just as Sara was going to call out to Dr. Schiller, the doctor lifted a finger to his lips and lightly moved his head from side to side, hopefully to ward off any acknowledgement on their part that would give them away to Bartholomew.

Sara looked around and saw a large man standing back and to one side and thought that perhaps he was the reason Dr. Schiller was acting strangely. She nudged Tyler and whispered in his ear, "Someone is following Dr. Schiller, it seems, so let's just walk up behind Dr. Schiller in line and pretend we don't know him."

The two teens did just that and as they stood closely to the good doctor he whispered over his shoulder to them, "That VA guy is here so we are going to have to change our plans. Tyler, what kind of a car do you have?"

"A '78 Ford 150 pick-up."

"Good. Best powertrain out there. Can it get you two to Massachusettes?"

"Does a hillbilly like cornbread?"

Dr. Schiller started laughing and then had to restrain himself, afraid of giving himself away. "After I get my ticket, I need for you to follow discreetly behind me to the restroom. Give me a couple of minutes headstart."

"Yes sir, I'll do that."

Dr. Schiller stepped up to the counter and spoke to the clerk and then turned away from the counter and walked toward the restroom. Not knowing what else to do, Tyler and Sara stepped up to the counter and Tyler asked, "Could you tell me where the men's restroom is?"

After getting directions Tyler walked off as Sara found herself a place to sit and wait, all the while keeping an eye on the VA man.

In the restroom, Tyler met with Dr. Schiller, "Tyler, did you see that big guy standing off behind us at the ticket desk?" Tyler nodded his head that he had seen the man. Dr. Schiller continued, "That's the VA guy. That man is not going to allow us to get on the plane together, and my guess is he will probably follow me on, so here is what I want you to do." Handing Tyler a credit card, Dr. Schiller continued, "Here is my credit card. You two kids get in your truck and head out for Massachusetts. Do you think you can do that? Use the card for whatever you need: gas; food; motels, whatever. Don't hesitate and don't drive too long before stopping. I will meet you at the military cemetery in Stow, Massachusetts. I figure it will take you several days and here is my business card with my cell phone number and some other numbers you will need on the back. If you have any problems, you call me. I will wait up there. When you arrive in Boston you call and let me know. I hate to do this, but this man can cause us a big problem and I don't need those kinds of problems and neither do you kids. Now, any questions?" Tyler shook his head 'no'. Dr. Schiller continued, "Tell Sara I'll call her folks and explain the situation."

Tyler looked at the cards in his hand and shook his head up and down knowing Sara would be worried.

"Good, then go and get Sara and head out while I keep that guy busy. I don't suppose you kids have had any breakfast?"

Tyler shook his head in the negative.

"Then start out by getting something to eat. Go now, get going, time's a' wasting."

Tyler tucked the cards in his pocket and headed out the door ahead of Dr. Schiller. As Tyler walked out the restroom door he almost had a head-on collision with Bartholomew who had decided to check up on the good doctor. "'Scuse me, sir," Tyler said as he tipped his hat toward the man he now knew to be their adversary.

Once he found Sara, now sitting on a bench near the Delta desk, he sat next to her and explained the change in the plan telling her they had to leave right away. Once outside Tyler told Sara that Dr. Schiller would call her mother and explain the change in plans. "But Tyler, can your truck make it that far?"

"Well, if'n it don't, Dr. Schiller told me to use his credit card for whatever we need, so if we have to get repairs, rent a car or buy a new one, then we will."

Once in the truck, Tyler headed out from the parking lot. At the ticket gate, the attendant looked at the ticket and told Tyler, "This was the long term parking. You haven't even been here an hour, but I have to charge you for the daily rate. Sorry, buddy."

Tyler handed over the credit card, "No sweat, man." He looked at Sara's disapproving frown. "Heck, we'll have to start sometime, might as well be now. I don't have that kind of money on me."

Tyler pulled out the exit and headed up the highway toward the interstate.

"Tyler, do you know where to go?"

"No, we'll get a map when we stop for gas," Looking at his gas gauge, "Which won't be long."

They headed up the highway going north until they saw signs for "Interstate 10". At the interchange they pulled into a gas station filling up the tank and purchasing a road atlas. Then they pulled into the McDonalds and ate some breakfast leaving when they were finished with a couple of cups of coffee.

Heading east they followed the highway until it intersected with "Interstate 95" in Jacksonville. Turning north they now considered themselves on their way.

"Tyler, does this make us fugitives?" Sara asked.

Tyler scrunched up his face a little as he thought about it, "Well, I don't know. I wouldn't say that we were exactly the Bonnie and Clyde types, but I suppose, if that VA guy wanted to get nasty..." Tyler didn't finish his sentence.

"Next time we stop, I'd better call my mom because I don't think we're gonna make it back by Sunday. I don't think we're even going to make it to Massachusetts by Sunday." Sara had been studying the map and knew that their distance to Jacob's burial place was over eleven hundred miles.

"Tyler, how many miles can we make a day?"

"I don't know. I've never driven this far so I don't know what my endurance is. But that also depends on if you can drive any."

"Tyler, I don't know how to drive."

"Your mom or dad hasn't shown you how to drive yet?"

"Tyler, I just turned fifteen, remember? I haven't had time to get my learner's permit yet."

"Oh, yeah, I forgot."

Sara rolled her eyes, "Boys," she mumbled.

"Well, if push comes to shove, I'll show you how to drive. Hope you can manage a stick shift."

"What's to manage, I've watched you drive. I can do it."

"Well, sayin' and doin' are two different things."

Sara looked at Tyler, with a less than happy expression, let out a "Humph" and then turned her attention to the country outside that was rapidly disappearing into the oncoming darkness.

"Tyler, we'd better look for someplace to stop for the night. We can get an early start tomorrow."

At the next interchange they pulled into a motel and got a room with two beds. As they walked into the room, Tyler laughed lightly, "When I asked for a room with two beds, the guy looked at me kind'a funny so I told him I was driving my sister to a fancy school up north and we didn't want to share a bed. That satisfied him."

Meanwhile, back at the airport as Dr. Schiller headed for the boarding gate for his flight, he noticed that Mr. Bartholomew had stopped, confused as to what to do and where to go, and then he disappeared. Once Dr. Schiller was on the plane he walked up and down the aisle and saw that the man was not on the flight.

Convinced that the man had given up, Dr. Schiller settled into his seat and readied himself for his trip. Little did Dr. Schiller know that Mr. Bartholomew had figured out what was going on and headed to his car, driving the same route as Sara and Tyler, not really knowing what kind of vehicle he was looking for, but aware of the young people that had been standing at the airport with Dr. Schiller.

Mr. Bartholomew continued driving following Tyler's and Sara's exact route almost as if he was a blood hound only the VA man continued on past where Sara and Tyler had stopped for the night. The man drove on for another fifty miles finally pulling off at the Red Oak exit. He knew he was on a wild goose chase, but felt he had no choice. He had to prevent a serious wrong doing in his eyes and in the eyes of the law.

The two teens awoke to find Jacob sitting on the dresser watching them, patiently waiting for them to awaken.

Sara opened her eyes to see Jacob staring at her. "Good morning, Jacob," she said, "What time is it?"

"It is just daylight and time to be on our way."

Tyler heard Sara talking and opened his eyes to see Jacob looking at Sara with tender eyes. He let his head drop heavily on his pillow and groaned, "Come on you guys. I need to sleep at least a little bit longer."

"Come on, Tyler, Jacob has a good point. We need to be on our way. Dr. Schiller will be waiting for us in Stow. We have a long way to go."

Tyler groaned again and then leaned forward on his elbows, "Okay, okay, but will you please look the other way while I get up and get my pants on?"

"Oh, for cryin' out loud, Tyler, I have a brother remember?"

"Yeah, but I'm not your brother and I don't have any sisters, so look the other way until I get my pants on."

Sara moaned and turned her head away from Tyler and looked instead toward Jacob, "I'd much rather look at Jacob anyway."

Sara and Tyler were on the road shortly after, not taking advantage of the motel's free breakfast. Jacob was riding shot gun in the cab. As they left the parking lot Tyler was bemoaning the fact that they couldn't even take long enough time for him to get a doughnut. "Geez, Sara, it's a free breakfast, just one doughnut or a sausage biscuit."

"Tyler, we can stop a little later and get something. Right now we've got to make some miles. Quit whining."

Tyler inhaled deeply and let his breath out with an exasperated air.

Sara looked at him with some attitude, "What'd you do, get out of the wrong side of the bed?"

"Not the wrong side just the wrong time."

"In other words, you're grumpy when you don't get enough sleep."

"Yes."

Sara turned and looked at Jacob, "Jacob, do you sleep, or even rest at all?"

"Sara, I have been sleeping, so to speak, for over a hundred years. It is not necessary for me to rest. I don't have a mortal body that needs replenishing so to eat or sleep is not necessary."

Sara felt stupid after asking a very stupid question so she just answered with a meek, "Oh."

After about an hour, Tyler looked at Sara, "Is it okay if we stop to eat something? My stomach thinks my throat's been cut."

With those words, Jacob leaned forward, "Are you injured, Tyler?"

Tyler laughed lightly, "No, Jacob, it's just a saying that means I'm hungry, really hungry."

With a smile, Sara answered Tyler, "Watch for a sign for the next McDonalds and pull off. We'll get something to go."

The next exit contained a McDonalds so Tyler took the exit and pulled in to the restaurant's parking lot, "Drive through or go inside?"

"Let's go inside." Sara answered, "That way there won't be any questions about Jacob." She turned toward Jacob, "You don't mind waiting in the truck do you, Jacob?"

"No, I will be fine here."

Sara and Tyler walked into the restaurant and up to the ordering counter, not really paying any attention to the other patrons seated around the restaurant, but someone there noticed them.

Mr. Bartholomew had decided to grab a bite to eat at the

McDonalds located right next to the motel where he had spent the night and was seated just inside the door that Sara and Tyler had just walked through. As he took a bite of his breakfast burrito he was looking directly at the door when the two teens walked in and literally froze his motion mid bite. *Those are the two that were with Schiller at the airport. And that kid, that's the one I almost walked into at the restroom. I can't believe my luck he* thought to himself. *Keep your head down so they don't see you.* Bartholomew dropped his head down looking only at the food in front of him, but his mind was going ninety miles an hour, *Keep your eyes peeled until they leave and then watch for their vehicle.*

Sara and Tyler got their food and Tyler pulled out Dr. Schiller's credit card and paid for the purchase, "We'd better fill up with gas before we get back on the interstate."

"You're the driver, do what has to be done," Sara replied.

As the two kids left the restaurant and headed for their truck, Bartholomew was watching out the corner of his eye, his head held down. Once the kids had walked out the glass doors, Bartholomew moved to the doors, waiting just inside, watching until the two had gotten into their truck. The VA man made a mental note of the make, model and color of the vehicle, but was not able to get a license number. *Good enough. I'll just stay on their tale until I can find a way to stop them.*

The one thing Bartholomew couldn't understand was the third figure he noticed sitting in the cab of the truck as it pulled out of the parking lot, *maybe a hitchhiker,* was how he explained the figure.

After filling the truck with gas, the kids moved out onto the highway again, heading north, a small white sedan following close behind them.

"Virginia is less than forty miles from here, Tyler. Then after Virginia is Washington D.C., then Maryland, Delaware, New Jersey, and then New York, Connecticut, Rhode Island and then Massachusetts." As she mentioned each state her level of excitement grew. When she said the latter she looked at Jacob sitting next to her and then a tiny tear trickled down her cheek which she quickly brushed away. "It won't be long, Jacob," she whispered to him.

"I didn't know we'd be taking a tour of the U.S." Tyler complained.

"Don't you ever look at a map or didn't you study geography."

"I don't pay much attention to that sort'a stuff."

"No wonder boys are so stupid" Sara mumbled to herself.

"Wha'd you say?"

"Nothing, just talking to Jacob," Sara answered and then she grew silent.

As the teens headed north on their mission, neither one noticed the white sedan that followed their every move. When they stopped for gas, the white sedan was nearby fueling up. When they stopped for food, the white sedan rolled through the drive thru right behind them. They had no reason to feel they were being followed or to fear for their mission.

As the hours flew by so did the miles. After about seven hours behind the wheel, Tyler was beginning to feel the lack of sleep and the long miles, "Sara, I need you to take over driving for a while."

Sara looked at Tyler, a frightened deer look to her eyes, "Tyler, I told you, I don't know how." Sara was defiant in her protestation.

"No time like the present to learn. Next gas stop or rest area you'll get your first lesson."

They were just approaching the New Jersey turnpike, "I sure wish we could have stopped in Washington D.C. for even a few hours," Sara whined.

"What the heck for?" Tyler asked.

"Tyler, for heaven's sakes, it isn't every day someone gets that close to our nation's capital. That is the center of our government. All of the important buildings, the Whitehouse, for cryin' out loud, are there. Haven't you ever wanted to visit those places?"

"I'd rather go fishin'."

In exasperation, Sara let out a huge puff of air and turned toward the window. Sensing her distress, Jacob gently put his arm around Sara's shoulders and she settled into him, or what she perceived to be him. Although others could see him he was still ethereal, but his presence was still comforting to her.

As their hours of travel sped by Tyler became more and more tired. At one point Sara noticed he was closing his eyes more and more often. "Tyler, we need to pull over and stop, you need to sleep."

Tyler looked over at her with his eyes barely open, "There is a service area coming up in five miles, I jus' saw the sign. We'll pull in there and get out an' stretch our legs, maybe get some coffee."

"Good, I'll call my mother and let her know we're still alive."

Within fifteen minutes, they were stopped at the gas pumps at the service area. Tyler crawled out of the driver's seat and hobbled over to the pump to start refueling, his legs stiff from staying in the same position for so many hours. Shoving the credit card into the pump, when the pump asked for additional information he pulled out the business card Dr. Schiller had given him and keyed in the required information that the good doctor had written on the back..

While Tyler was fueling the truck, Sara went inside and purchased a couple of cups of coffee with what little cash they had left. While inside she found a pay phone and placed a collect call to her home. When the phone was answered, it was her mom at the other end of the line and her hello sounded frantic. When given the go-ahead, they both tried to talk at once, "Sara, oh my god, are you all right?" Jean asked.

"Of course, Mom, I'm fine. We had to make some last minute changes…"

"I know, Dr. Schiller called and told me what happened. Sara, where are you?"

"I'm not exactly sure, Mom. We're on the New Jersey turnpike, somewhere."

"What did you do last night? You didn't drive all night, did you? Sara, you've got to be…"

"Mom, slow down and I'll tell you everything." Sara went on to explain their getaway from the airport and the trip thus far. When she told Jean that they had spent the night at a motel, Jean erupted,

"A motel? I hope you two got separate rooms?"

"Mom, Dr. Schiller is paying for all of this, of course we stayed in the same room. I'm not going to build up a huge bill for him…"

"You and Tyler stayed overnight in the same room?"

"And Jacob, and Mom, nothing happened. Tyler and I don't feel like that to each other. For heaven's sake, give me a break, Mom. He's more like my brother."

"What are you going to do tonight?"

"Probably the same thing. We'll get a room with two

beds and he'll sleep in one and I'll sleep in the other. Quite proper, Mom."

"This is insane. I wish I had not agreed to this fool-hardy scheme in the first place! Sara, I am so frightened…"

"Mom, chill out. Everything is alright. Nothing's happened. I'm okay and so is Tyler."

"Oh, Sara, you are so young…"

There was a pause and Sara could hear a change in her mother's voice and could tell she was starting to cry, "Mom, please don't worry. I'll be okay and so will Tyler. We are over half way there and everything is going just fine. Dr. Schiller is going to meet us in Stow and we're supposed to call him when we get into the Boston area." Sara had no idea they were being followed.

When she returned to the truck, Tyler was sitting back behind the wheel and Jacob had moved over to the middle. Sara climbed into the passenger side. None of them noticed the white sedan that had pulled into one of the other gas lanes or the man who was now pumping gas into the car.

Tyler pulled away from the pump and stopped the truck in the vast parking lot. He got out of the truck and walked over to the passenger side, opened the door and told Sara to get out.

"Get out?"

"Yes, you're gonna learn to drive. It's time you started to help with the driving chore."

"Tyler, I told you...?"

"Sara, no time like the present to learn. Go over and get behind the wheel." Sara felt a wave of anxiety wash over her as she followed Tyler's order. Once seated behind the wheel, she felt dwarfed by the immensity of the truck, something she had never felt before. She tried to put her feet on the pedals and found she had to slide way down in the seat to make contact with the instruments necessary to make the vehicle go. "Tyler, I won't be able to drive this thing, I can't reach the pedals."

"Move the seat."

"How do I do that?"

Tyler groaned, "There is a handle at the side by the door. Pull up on it and then the seat will move forward. Jacob and I will help."

Sara did as advised and the seat moved forward until her feet were firmly placed on the pedals. The motor was still running so Tyler gave her the next instructions, "Okay, now, with your left foot, push down the far left pedal and hold it there while you shift the lever into the lower position. Pull the lever toward you and then down toward the seat. Think of an H Sara. You're going to move the lever into the lower left of the H.

Sara did as she was told. She pushed the pedal with everything she had and held the pedal to the floor. Then she nervously moved the lever into the correct position.

"Now, this next move takes a little coordination. Put your

right foot on the gas pedal and as you push on the gas, let off with your left foot, not all of a sudden, but ease each one. Once you get the feeling you'll be able to do it faster. Okay, now go ahead and try it."

Sara pushed on the gas and the engine revved as she let up on the clutch pedal. The truck lurched forward with a thunk and the motor died. Tyler and Sara's heads snapped back with the sudden lurch of the vehicle.

Tyler leaned forward and looked past Jacob at Sara. "I said, gently."

Sara's eyes began to shine as a build-up of tears collected near the edges. "You said, 'ease', and that's what I did."

"Well then ease a little faster on the gas and a little slower on the clutch. Turn the key and try again."

Sara turned the key and as the motor revved up Tyler motioned with his hand downward for her to ease back on the gas which she did. "Now the transition from the clutch to the gas has to be subtle, but definitive."

"My, such big words, Tyler."

"Just do as I said, we need to get rolling. Once you get this thing moving, I'll tell you what to do next."

Sara made another attempt, this time she actually got the truck to roll ahead slightly before it lurched and died.

"Try again, Sara." Tyler was losing patience and it was

noticeable in his voice.

Sara applied an immense amount of concentration, her tongue sticking out of the side of her mouth as she bit it slightly. She turned the key, pressed in the clutch pedal and pressed on the gas pedal as she eased the clutch back out and the truck eased forward. "Give it a little more gas, Sara." Tyler urged.

Sara pressed on the pedal and the truck leapt forward. She was so focused on the pedals at her feet she forgot entirely about the steering wheel. "What now, Tyler, what do I do now?"

"Aim for the on ramp to the highway. Now get your speed up a little, press the clutch pedal...the left one, and move the gear shift lever up slightly and then over and up. Then give it some more gas."

Sara was wiggling her head back and forth, "Tyler, there's too much to do. I can't do it all."

"Sure you can, but let's take a turn around the parking lot before we head out on the highway. Turn up here at the next parking lane and make a big circle around the lot. I'll have you gear down and then back up again."

Sara followed Tyler's instructions and the truck made a scenic tour of the parking lot as the VA man watched the truck play merry-go-round. He sat in his white sedan as the truck went around, as if confused, to the point he wanted to get out and direct it onto the on ramp. He was about to get out of his car when the truck headed for the ramp. The man put his car in gear and moved out to catch up.

"Calm down, Sara, you're doing fine. Now get some more speed, get it up to forty, forty five and then shift again. Think of an 'H' and you are going down on the right side of the 'H'. Good girl, now we're on our way. Just keep the truck between the two lines and pointed toward the direction we are going now."

As the truck sped down the interstate Sara gained some confidence and settled into the seat. Tyler kept his eyes on the road for a while watching Sara weave between the lines as the other traffic sped past her, but with her adrenaline up Sara gained confidence as she gained more control of the wheel and became more comfortable, keeping the truck steadily in the lane.

"When you feel more comfortable, you can give it a little more gas and get it up to fifty-five. Then you want to keep it at fifty-five from then on."

"Okay. Tyler, I know you're tired and need to sleep, but please stay awake for a while, will ya? Just in case something happens."

"Okay, I'll stay awake as long as I can."

The teens settled into their seats for a long ride, but it didn't take long before Sara was tiring. Not used to driving and the nerve wracking start to her driving experience had brought on a case of lethargy. Her eyelids began to grow heavy and she became drowsy. Tyler had already figured that it was safe enough for him to drift off and was sound asleep, his head leaning against the passenger door window gently bobbing up and down with the surface of the road.

"Tyler, wake up." Sara called out to her companion.

"Tyler, wake up, I'm getting tired." Tyler neither batted an eyelid nor moved a muscle.

"Jacob, what am I gonna do. If Tyler doesn't take over, I'm going to fall asleep and then we'll crash. TYLER, WAKE UP!" Sara yelled, but her words were swallowed by the road noise and Tyler continued to sleep. Sara began to cry.

"Perhaps I can help, Sara," Jacob said.

"You, how can you help, Jacob? You've never driven a car."

No, that is true, but then until a short while ago, neither had you."

Contrite, Sara answered, "True."

"I was watching and listening as Tyler explained it to you and I believe I have an answer."

"What is it, Jacob."

Jacob hesitated for a brief moment and then said, "I can slide into you and help keep you awake, or you can sleep while I drive using your body. Remember, I don't need sleep, so I won't fall asleep."

Sara thought about it for a brief second and then asked, "What do I have to do?"

"Nothing, just sit there. It is all up to me."

Sara was apprehensive but desperate. "Okay, let's do it."

"Just focus on the road ahead and don't pay any attention to me."

Sara looked forward out to the road in front of her and did not look at all at Jacob. Jacob's seemingly solid body took on a misty appearance and then it seemed as if he disappeared into Sara.

Sara shuddered slightly, as if a cold chill had taken over, and then she sat up straighter with a more firm hold on the steering wheel. A mixture of emotions enveloped her. She felt a confidence she had not felt before, a self assuredness yet a deeper sense of vulnerability.

"Jacob, are you there?"

"Yes, Sara, I'm here." The words were mere thoughts in Sara's mind, not actual words that she heard. She felt as if she had no control. Her movements seemed to happen automatically as if someone else was in control. Thinking for only a fraction of a second she thought, *well, actually, someone else is in control.* Her foot pressed a little harder on the gas pedal and the truck responded with speed. *Tyler said to keep it at fifty-five.* "I'm sorry I lost my focus while we were trading places."

"We didn't really trade places, Sara, I am inside you."

"Oh, yeah, this is gonna take a little getting used to."

Behind them, the VA man, Bartholomew, was rubbing his eyes, not sure of what he had just seen through the rear window of the truck ahead of him. As he trailed behind the truck, he was able to make out the three individuals riding in the cab. One of the males had moved over and was leaning against the passenger door, probably sleeping. The girl was driving, which would explain the bizarre behavior in the parking lot, but the second male had been sitting in-between the other two, and then he wasn't. After rubbing his eyes, Bartholomew shook his head as if to remove the cobwebs from long hours behind the wheel, but he had not imagined that third rider and he did not imagine his sudden disappearance and there was certainly no where for him to go in the cab of that pick-up. Bartholomew took a deep breath and let it out as he leaned into his steering wheel and his thoughts ran to *I'm getting too old for this nonsense.*

After a few minutes of their dual driving Tyler's eyelids fluttered and he woke up. Looking over toward Sara, he jumped in his seat, startled awake and disoriented by what he didn't see. "Sara, where's Jacob?" After hours of riding between the two teens, Tyler was surprised to see Jacob gone.

Two voices replied from the same mouth, "I am here" and "He's here." emerged from Sara's lips at the same time. Tyler looked confused. "What's goin' on or am I dreamin'?"

Sara smiled at his confusion, "You're not dreaming and that'll teach you to fall asleep when you told me you would stay awake."

Tyler scratched his head, "I don't understand. Where's Jacob?"

"Tyler, he is here, in me."

"Wha...?"

"I got so tired I couldn't stay awake and I tried to wake you only you wouldn't. So Jacob came up with a solution. He is in me. He de-materialized and in mist form he entered my body. He doesn't need to sleep so when I get tired he can take over my body and drive while you and I both sleep. He knows how to drive by watching you teach me. Tyler, it is so cool. You have no idea. I don't even need to talk to him. All I have to do is think what I want him to know and he knows it and it is the same with him. I don't hear him talk; I just hear his words as thoughts in my head."

"I'm not sure I like this."

"Why not, it's the perfect solution."

"Yeah, well, I think we'd better pull off at the next service area. I noticed they have motels, so we don't need to leave the turnpike. There should be a service area coming up soon. They are usually about every fifty miles or so. When you see a sign for the next one, wake me up."

"Yeah, easier said than done," Sara was beginning to doubt Tyler's word.

Within fifteen minutes they passed a sign that indicated a service area coming up. Sara reached over and shoved on Tyler while she called out to him, "Tyler, service area coming up.

He jerked awake and straightened himself as Sara slowed into the exit ramp, "Sara, use your brake to slow down until you are at about forty miles per hour, then push in on the clutch pedal and gear down, that is move your gear shift up to second, the upper H and then let out on the clutch. Second gear will kick in and it will help you decelerate. Then when you are down to about twenty miles, do it again only go down to first, the lower left side of the H and when you are ready to stop push on the brake pedal, the middle one, and the clutch at the same time. And glide to a stop."

With Jacob in control, so to speak, Sara followed the instructions to the letter. The pick-up glided to a stop in one of the parking spaces. Sara smiled broadly when they were stopped, *"We make a pretty good team, Jacob." "Yes, indeed we do."* The thought made Sara smile.

Tyler looked at Sara, a broad smile on his face, "Well, Sara, you pulled it off. Ah didn't know for sure if having you drive was a good idea, but you did it, and not one dent in mah fender."

Sara looked at Tyler with a disappointed expression, "Oh ye of little faith."

When they stepped out of the truck Sara and Tyler grabbed their duffel bags and Sara grabbed her backpack and they headed for the building where the Howard Johnson sign indicated there was a motel. Sara walked with a much more masculine stride.

Once they secured their room they moved quickly. It was only eight o'clock, but they were each worn out and ready for bed.

In their room Sara and Tyler flipped a coin to see who would get to shower first. Tyler won so he disappeared into the bathroom. Sara in the meantime turned on the television and flopped onto the bed ready to sleep.

On the television was "Gone With The Wind" and as Sara settled down to watch the movie, and perhaps sleep a few winks, Jacob had other ideas. As Sara's eyes slowly drifted closed, "This is nonsense." Jacob declared as he watched the action on the small screen. Sara's eyes popped open. Toward the end of the film as the Union soldiers were pillaging the plantations Jacob became outraged, "Our soldiers did not behave in such a beastly manner."

"Jacob, sad to say, they did. The south was ravaged by the northern troops. The people were left without food or proper clothes and many died. The Union was not kind to the civilians who were not soldiers. As a matter of fact, General Sherman burned his way across Georgia, destroying everything in his wake. Many of the grand plantation homes were burned to the ground leaving their residents homeless."

"It is shameful." Jacob seemed deep in thought, "How is it that we can sit here and watch this happening when this happened many years ago?" Jacob was confused.

"Jacob, this is a movie; made in our time to depict that time. Do you understand?"

"No, but I will take your explanation."

All of this discussion was taking place without words because Jacob's spirit was still inside Sara and their words were flying back and forth in her mind, mere thoughts rather than spoken words.

Suddenly Sara thought of her upcoming shower. "Jacob, I think it might be wise for you to take your ghostly form. It isn't necessary for you to still be inside me."

"Yes, I agree. It isn't difficult for me, but to stay in this form, inside you, I am sure cannot be easy for you. Just lie down and relax and I will remove myself."

Sara lay back on the bed and closed her eyes. Her body shuddered slightly as Jacob withdrew his ethereal form and drifted above Sara's mortal form. Jacob was hovering there when Tyler walked out of the bathroom.

Tyler stopped suddenly; dropping the towel he was still holding to his head to dry his hair. His mouth fell open as he looked at Jacob hovering over Sara as a rain cloud hovers over a field. "Sara, what's goin' on?"

Sara had almost fallen asleep, she was so tired, and jerked awake when Tyler spoke. "Jacob was just removing himself from me. Why?"

Tyler hesitated a bit, not sure what to say. He didn't want to appear jealous or worried or anything else for that matter. "Just wanted to let you know the shower is now yours."

"Thanks Tyler, I just thought it best that Jacob free himself from my body before I got into the shower, know what I mean?"

Embarrassed by the possibilities, Tyler agreed. "We'd better go get something to eat and then get some sleep. I'm beat."

"Tyler, why don't you go get us something and bring it back to the room. Just get me a burger and fries and something to drink. You should know what I like by now."

"Okay, I'll be back in a few minutes. You get your shower and we can eat when I get back."

Tyler found his way down to the restaurant portion of the 'Howard Johnson's' and placed an order. While he was standing at the order counter, he didn't see Bartholomew checking in at the motel registration. Before Tyler's food was ready, Mr. Bartholomew entered the men's restroom so that as Tyler made his way through the lobby and back to the room he was unaware of the VA man's presence.

Bartholomew knew the kids were there because he had seen their truck out in the parking lot. As a matter of fact he had driven through the lot until he spotted their truck then he decided to stay.

After coming out of the restroom, he went to his room and then came back down and sat in the restaurant and ate.

After her shower Sara actually felt human again. She

came out of the bathroom combing her hair. Jacob was sitting on her bed and smiled as she walked over to where he was sitting and sat next to him. "Jacob, we are almost there. We are only a few hundred miles from your home."

"Sara, that is wonderful. I really don't know how to thank you."

"I know Jacob, I'm just happy that you felt comfortable enough to first materialize in front of me."

"I felt a closeness to you, Sara, that I have never felt with anyone else. As I said before, you and I are kindred spirits, and I believe we will remain close forever. I will always be near you, Sara."

Sara had felt the tears getting closer and wanted to end their conversation before she ended up a blubbering fool. Just as the tears were about to tip over the rims of her eyes, Tyler walked through the door. "Dinner is served." He lifted the tray containing the food as if to show it off, and then sat it on the table. Sara moved quickly to sit at the table wiping the tears from her eyes as she moved.

Tyler, noticing the redness of Sara's eyes, asked her, "Everything okay, Sara?"

"Yes, I'm fine, just talking to Jacob about getting him home."

Tyler did something very uncharacteristic for him, he reached over and put his arm over Sara's shoulder and squeezed her lightly, "Everything is going to be just fine, Sara. You wait and see." And then he smiled at her, a loving, brotherly smile.

The next morning, just before daybreak, Bartholomew was up and out in his car waiting for the two teens to leave. With a large cup of coffee to keep awake, he was just taking a drink when he spotted the two leaving the motel. He slid down slightly in his seat to be less obvious and then watched as the two proceeded to their truck carrying two duffel bags and a backpack.

He was about to take another swallow of his coffee when the two kids reached their truck. The boy went to the driver's side and slung the two duffel bags, which he was carrying, into the back of the truck, and the girl went to the passenger side where she stopped. She was carrying the backpack and she waited by the door presumably waiting for the boy to unlock it.

While he watched, Bartholomew took another drink of his coffee. Suddenly, as he watched, a mist formed, seemingly coming from the backpack and a third entity appeared. Bartholomew jerked, startled, and began to choke on his coffee, spraying it all over the interior of his car. As he coughed and sputtered, the girl and the other figure he had seen the night before climbed into the truck. The engine roared into life and the truck was soon moving out of the service area, once again heading north. Bartholomew regained his composure and got his car moving and was soon tailing the teens once again.

The truck was soon moving along at a good speed and Bartholomew had to pay attention in order to keep up with his quarry, not like the night before when the girl had been driving.

They sped along the New Jersey turnpike and were soon approaching New York City. Sara was navigating, alerting Tyler to any upcoming interchanges that might need attention. "Just follow the signs for Interstate 95, Tyler. We stay on I-95 all the way to Boston."

As they approached, crossing over into Manhattan, Sara bemoaned the fact that they wouldn't be taking a tunnel into the city, "I sure wish we were taking the Lincoln tunnel into Manhattan."

"Why aren't we?" Tyler wondered.

"Because that would take us directly into downtown Manhattan and that we don't need. I-95 follows across the George Washington Bridge and goes through upper Manhattan non-stop. No traffic problems."

"Then we'll stay on I-95." The bridge was a toll bridge and Tyler pulled out the doctor's credit card to pay and then they were on their way. Unfortunately, it was morning rush hour and the traffic crossing over the bridge and through their next stretch of the interstate was heavily congested. It was, after all, Monday morning and New Yorkers were on their way to work.

Tyler tried to hold his jangled nerves in check amongst the frantic motorists, but was soon at the end of his rope, "Was this the only way we could have come?" he asked Sara angrily. "Couldn't you have found us a more remote way to come?"

"Tyler, this is New York. What did you expect? At least we avoided downtown, as much as I would have loved seeing it."

Jacob looked at the mass of humanity and machines surrounding them and remarked frantically, "This is not the New York I remember."

Sara looked at Jacob, "Yes, Jacob, but when were you here?"

Jacob seemed to think about it and then stated, "Eighteen sixty. It was my first trip out and we came here after leaving Boston."

"How old were you?"

"I was twelve, but... there was nothing like this." Jacob was moving his head from side to side, looking at the passing cars and trucks and the high graffiti covered concrete walls separating the freeway and the buildings just beyond the walls.

As they were listening to Jacob's explanation, Sara realized that an important interchange was coming so she spoke, interrupting Jacob, "I'm sorry, Jacob. Tyler, there is an important interchange coming up. Follow the signs for I-95 and that will lead us to the New England Thruway. I'm sure it will also mention Boston, so keep your eyes peeled for any mention of those on the signs."

Still the kids had no idea of the white sedan that had been following them since early this morning. Tyler, instead of looking behind him was paying much more attention to the confusion around and ahead of him.

The VA man in the white sedan stayed with the truck and paid close attention to the surrounding traffic. With all of the traffic, their progress had slowed down considerably and he was concerned that he would be detected, but it seemed that his vehicle was invisible because never once did it appear to him that he had been discovered by the traveling teens.

The traffic thinned out some as they neared the outskirts of The Bronx and then moved through New Rochelle. Soon after they saw signs for Connecticut. "Gentlemen, we are now out of New York," Sara said with a smile of confidence as if their troubles were all over, but as they moved east, the traffic continued to remain much heavier than they were used to.

"Sara, do you realize it has taken us two hours to go barely over twenty-two miles?" Tyler was frustrated with their progress.

Even as she watched their progression on the map, little did Sara realize that the amount of humanity did not decrease with distance from New York, but continued on a steady course following the Atlantic seaboard all the way from New York until they reached Boston.

Once again Sara made mention of those things they were by-passing on their trip, "Tyler, do you have any idea how much history we have been passing. What I mean is, this whole area saw the beginning of our country. How I would love to be able to stop and see some of the historic places.

Tyler more or less ignored her comments and Sara could tell she was being ignored, "Tyler, are you ignoring me?"

"Sara, I'm not interested in the historic sites. We are not on a vacation. Have you forgotten why we are here in the first place?"

Sara looked up into Jacob's face, "Of course not. I was just thinking out loud… Tyler, don't you have any romantic blood in you?"

"What's romantic about history? I get enough of that in school."

The three passengers in the truck moved onward in silence.

By this time they were entering into Rhode Island, "One more state and, Jacob, you will be home."

Jacob looked into Sara's eyes and smiled softly, "Thank you, Sara."

Yankee Boy

Chapter Twenty Six

They reached the outskirts of Boston by early evening. They were tired, but ready to get their trip over with. A light rain had started which made the driving more hazardous.

Tyler was still driving and was becoming weary so as they approached their turnoff for the most direct route to Stow, despite Sara's warning, Tyler missed the turnoff. Angry and upset he turned on Sara, "Dang it, Sara, you didn't call that soon enough. I wasn't prepared. Now I have to get off the interstate and come back."

"Tyler, don't yell at me. I gave you plenty of warning. You just didn't listen. Let me look and see if there is an alternative route, but don't yell at me. That was your fault. You weren't paying attention."

Sara was correct. She had given him fair warning, but in his driving daze, Tyler was not paying attention and became confused when Sara called out the turn. He was in the wrong lane and could not get to the exit in time.

Sara looked at the map with a flashlight and realized that there was another route. "Tyler, if we take I-95 all the way into

Boston we can take another exit and follow a two lane highway to Stow. And from the exit, it looks like it is only…" Sara paused as she added up the miles, "Fifteen miles or so to Stow.

"Once we get onto a northward track I'll tell you the exit to watch for."

They drove further and once again they hit the inner-city area during rush hour, but luckily for them, the bulk of the traffic was going out of the city. They followed I-95 and when it took a course that seemed to circle the downtown area, Sara stated, "Watch for the Waltham, Weston exit, Highway 20, and for heaven's sake, Tyler, stay in the outside lane so we don't miss this exit."Tyler did as Sara said and soon they were westbound on Highway 20. "Now, watch for Highway 27 leading off to the right. There might even be a sign for Stow."

Once they spotted their turn, Sara suggested they pull into a gas station to use the phone, "We need to call Dr. Schiller and let him know where we are."

Calling Dr. Schiller's number, the man answered, "Sara, good to hear from you two. Where are you, I was beginning to get worried."

"We're okay, Dr. Schiller, we're only about fifteen miles from Stow. We missed our turnoff for I-495 so we had to follow I-95 and we are about to drive up Highway 27 so it's only fifteen miles according to the map."

"Have you kids eaten yet?"

"No."

"My treat when you get here. Have you called your mother, recently?"

"Not since two nights ago."

"I'll give her a call and let her know that things are going well. I'll see you kids in about thirty minutes."

"Okay, Dr. Schiller, see you soon."

As she got back into the truck, Sara asked, "Tyler, you've been driving all day. Don't you want me to drive some?"

"That's okay, Sara, we're not that far. I can get us there."

"But Tyler, you're tired, I can tell. Maybe you should let me…"

"Sara, "Tyler said curtly, "I said I'm okay. It's only fifteen miles. I can do that in my sleep."

"I hope so, because you look to me like you are asleep. Please let me drive."

"Sara, I'll manage. I'll open the window if I get tired. The air is cold enough, that'll keep me awake. You just sit and keep Jacob company."

Sara turned her attention to the window and resolutely folded her arms across her chest as she mumbled, "Boys!"

Neither of the teens had noticed the white sedan that

had followed them off of the interstate and was now following them on their last miles to their destination.

Within five miles the two kids were on a narrow two lane scenic highway heading for Stow, Massachusetts, Jacob's birthplace. The white car was right behind them. It was dark, the road was curvy and the light mist that had been falling was turning to ice on the road. Slowing to gain more control, Tyler looked over to Sara as they slid lightly on a curve, "Now, aren't you glad I didn't let you drive?"

Sara's eyes, even in the dark, glowed with fear, the whites showing brightly in the greenish glare of the dash lights. "Tyler, what is going on?"

"The wet highway has iced over. I've got to be extremely careful."

Inside the white car, Bartholomew was watching the progression of events and decided that he had to stop those kids. Long hours behind the wheel and his concern for the law, made the government man's thinking turn irrational. *It was time they knew that the law was on to them and stop whatever travesty they are about to commit*, he thought. He had missed several opportunities to confront them along the way, so his irrational mind decided now would be his only chance. The only problem was that Bartholomew was unaware of the road conditions; he was so focused on stopping the teens.

Suddenly, inside the truck, their heads snapped back as the car behind them bumped their rear bumper. As Tyler fought for control of the truck, Sara looked out the back window and saw a large man sitting at the wheel of the white sedan behind them. The car backed off again and then sped up and bumped their rear bumper again. With the second bump, Sara screamed, "Tyler, he's doing it on purpose. What is going on?"

"I don't know, Sara, I don't know." The car bumped them again. Tyler was focusing all of his attention on keeping the truck under control.

As the car approached to strike them a fourth time, Sara screamed, "He's coming at us again."

Despite the ice, Tyler pressed on the gas pedal, "Hang on, Sara, I'm gonna try and outrun this guy. "You got your seat belt on?"

"Yes," Sara squeaked out, holding the backpack tightly to her chest.

As Tyler sped up, so did the white car. Bartholomew's mind was racing, *so they're gonna try and outrun me, huh? Well, we'll just see.* The VA man stepped on his accelerator and began to move to the left into the oncoming lane; his intent was to pass the truck and get in front to slow them down. As he pulled out from behind the truck, Tyler saw what was going on and let his foot off the gas pedal. The deceleration, just as Bartholomew began to pass, caused his car to strike its right front fender against the rear fender of the truck. All of this happened as they moved into a curve on the road that neither driver had seen coming.

The impact sent both vehicles out of control on the icy

highway. Tyler lost control and shot off the curve and as the truck sped off the highway, the passenger side dropped off the edge of the pavement and put the truck into a position to roll. The truck flipped several times as it traveled down the icy slope next to the highway throwing Tyler out and away from the descending vehicle.

With no traction on the icy pavement Bartholomew's car rotated from the impact, and slammed into a nearby tree, projecting the huge man out through the windshield and into the woods below.

As the two vehicles settled and the smoke cleared, there was stillness in the night. No sound but a spinning wheel could be heard in the forested scene that had been ravaged by man's machines.

There was a subtle movement near the truck as Jacob, already a ghost, moved out of the mangled truck unharmed. He turned and reached his hand to help Sara, now a mere specter of her former self, climb out of the wreckage.

Sara looked at Jacob and then back at her mortal body lying in the wreckage, her seatbelt still tight against her body, "Jacob? ... What happened?"

"An accident, Sara, but I have you."

Sara looked at Jacob, "But that's me, yet I am here," Sara started to cry, "What happened, Jacob, what happened?" Sara reached out to embrace Jacob and this time did not embrace air. Sara continued to cry.

Jacob reached over and lifted Sara's chin with his fingers, "Sara, you are like me now. But don't be sad, I will care for you." Jacob paused slightly, "I will care for you forever."

Sara smiled softly, "I know Jacob, I know. Where's Tyler?"

"He's nearby, but he will live."

Sara cried harder, "Oh, this is going to be hard."

"Believe me, Sara, it is very easy."

"No, Jacob, that's not what I mean. This is going to be hard for my family." Sara cried more tears, not for herself, but for her family.

Jacob looked into Sara's eyes and smiled, a warm and loving smile, "Sara, trust me and I will take care of you. Think about this, now we can be together... always."

Sara returned his smile, "I love you, Jacob, and I do trust you... forever."

Jacob took Sara's hand and pulled her back toward the overturned truck and then the two spirits disappeared into the backpack of bones.

Nearby, up the slope that the truck had tumbled down, Tyler lay in an unconscious heap. As the truck screamed over the edge into the black abyss, he was thrown out, barely damaged, as the truck rolled away from him.

After some time Tyler regained consciousness and sat up.

Although disoriented, he soon collected himself when he looked down at his mangled truck just a few yards from where he sat. When some form of rational thought finally settled into Tyler's brain he remembered what had happened and his first thought was of Sara. "Sara, Saaraa," he called but he received no answer.

He stood, unsteady on his feet, and moved gently down the slope to his truck, calling Sara's name constantly, "Saaraa, Saaraa, oh, Saaraa," now it was Tyler who was crying as he moved around to the other side of the truck. As he approached the passenger side Tyler was able to look into the overturned vehicle and saw Sara's lifeless body still clutching the backpack.

"Oh, Sara," Tears were streaming down Tyler's face as he realized that Sara was dead. He reached out and touched her battered face, "Oh, Sara." He staggered back and fell into the snow, distraught over the result of his decisions: to help Sara on her quest; and more recently, to challenge the driver of the white car. *Why...oh why? Why this? If only I could go back in time, I would change everything,* were Tyler's thoughts, *why Sara, why not me...why not me?* Tyler collapsed in a mound of guilt and remorse; with each sob the word *why?* echoed through his mind.

Then Tyler could hear Sara's voice. Well, he didn't really hear it. It was more like a thought; *"Take the backpack to Dr. Schiller."* Tyler looked around, somehow hoping that it wasn't Sara that he was seeing in the battered truck. Hearing her voice he looked around hoping to find her somewhere outside the truck. *"Tyler, take the backpack to Dr. Schiller."* Tyler looked around again and then squeaked out a reply to Sara, "Sara, where are you?"

"Tyler, I'm with Jacob. Please, take the backpack to Dr. Schiller. You must get the backpack to him."

"Sara, You're in the..." Tyler couldn't continue, he broke down crying, collapsing into the snow-covered hillside.

"Tyler, I'm dead. My spirit is with Jacob. You must take the backpack to Dr. Schiller. Tell him what happened. It is important that he finish with our task."

"But Sara..."

"No buts, Tyler, you must take this to the end. Don't worry about me. I will be fine. I'm with Jacob, and he will take care of me."

Tyler started to cry out, "Saaraa, please, come back..."

"Tyler, please, finish our task, I'm depending on you. We both are. Now, take the backpack to Dr. Schiller, please. And Tyler, one more thing, please see that I am buried next to Jacob, please." Sara was pleading with Tyler.

Tyler stood and then walked over to the demolished pickup truck. He reached in through the shattered window and grasped the backpack with his one functioning arm and withdrew it from Sara's arms then he made his way back up to the road and started walking toward Stow.

In Stow, Dr. Schiller was keeping his eye on the time,

anticipating the arrival of the kids. His watch ticked past the thirty minutes and still no kids. When an hour had ticked by Dr. Schiller decided to act. Considering the weather and the long hours the kids had been driving, he headed away from Stow and toward highway twenty-seven.

The road was dark and dangerous and Dr. Schiller had an ominous feeling in his gut as he drove away from Stow.

About four miles after he turned onto highway twenty-seven, Dr. Schiller spotted a familiar figure walking with an unsteady gait along the shoulder of the highway. As quickly as he could safely stop his car, Dr. Schiller rolled down his window and shouted, "Tyler, for God's sake, where is Sara? What happened?"

Tyler was already crying and when Dr. Schiller mentioned Sara's name, he blubbered even harder. Pointing down the highway behind him, Tyler blabbered on about "a white car, a man, an accident, and Sara... Sara... oh, Dr. Schiller, Sara's dead and all for a dang bag of bones!" Tyler held up the backpack and shook it.

Tyler fell into Dr. Schiller's arms as he broke down entirely, crying beyond comforting.

Dr. Schiller helped Tyler into the car and laid him down on the back seat. "I'll get you to a hospital, son. But I need to check Sara first."

Dr. Schiller got into his car and moved slowly forward down the highway until he spotted some skid marks in the ice and indentations in the ice and snow covered weeds at the edge of the pavement. He stopped his car and then moved it again so that he could use the headlights to illuminate the scene below.

The doctor moved down over the edge and made his way down to the truck. He moved over to where he spotted Sara's body and touched her neck searching for a pulse. Finding none, he too allowed a tear to trickle down his cheek. "I am so sorry, Sara; so sorry." Remorse and despair overcame Dr. Schiller as he dropped his head, a couple of tears sliding down his face.

Dr. Schiller took out his cell phone and dialed 911 to report the accident. As he disconnected the call he noticed the other car Tyler had mentioned and moved over to it. Out beyond the overturned car, Dr. Schiller saw a form lying in a heap. He made his way over to the form and realized it was the VA man. Reaching down, Dr. Schiller once more checked for a pulse. Finding none he stood defiantly and stated, "Serves you right, you S.O.B."

Chapter Twenty Seven

A week later a solemn ceremony was begun in the military section of the Stow Cemetery.

The small group of civilians stood nearby. Jean, Jack, and Eddie Richardson, their faces red from tears, watched as the final moments of the service were conducted. With special permission, Sara had been buried next to where Jacob's remains were now being interred. Jean and Jack, with some trepidation, but acting according to Sara's wishes, had consented to the burial of their daughter in this distant place.

Dr. Schiller stood quietly, Tyler standing to his right, as a box holding Jacob's bones was slowly lowered into the hole. A soldier from a local re-enactors group played "Taps" as seven Union re-enactors stood at attention, rifles shouldered. Dr. Schiller had made arrangements for the military style proceedings in advance of their trip.

The gravesite was located in an obscure corner of the cemetery now considered obsolete; a memorial to those from Stow who had fought in the War Between the States stood nearby and the rest of the markers were nearly faded.

As the box bottomed out in the grave in the ancient cemetery grounds, the rifles echoed out a tribute to the fallen soldier. Then the assembled re-enactors, each wearing a canteen and a black arm band, took the canteens and each drank a swallow from the vessels and then stepped forward and poured the remainder of the water into the grave. Retreating from the grave they once more stood at attention and saluted the fallen soldier. As Tyler and Dr. Schiller watched the final moments of the ceremony, Dr. Schiller wrapped his arm around Tyler's shoulder and squeezed ever so slightly.

The teenager stood quietly until the given moment and then he stepped forward and began to un-wrap a large package brought from Florida by the Richardson family that had been lying on the ground near the edge of the grave. When the wrappings fell away the large stone that had marked Jacob's grave in Florida lay at his feet. But now the stone was different; the moss had been cleaned off and the three slash marks had been covered by a bronze plaque noting Jacob's name, his birth and death dates and his military unit.

Tyler picked up the heavy stone and stepped forward to move it to the head of the grave where it would stand for all times. Then Tyler returned to his place with the others beside the grave.

As Tyler watched the proceedings, he looked across the opening in the ground and saw Jacob standing near the edge. Jacob was looking down at the box as it lay in the bottom of the hole. What Tyler saw next shook him to his core yet it pleased him on a different level. Sara materialized next to Jacob and then Jacob placed his arm around her shoulder. On Sara's face was a soft contented smile and then she raised her hand and waved at Tyler.

Jack and Jean looked numbly at the graves, their grief so devastating they were unable to see the two spirits standing next to the pit.

As Tyler watched, Sara's ghost then disappeared and reappeared next to Jean. Jean raised her head as Sara seemed to whisper something in her ear. What Jean heard, not as words, but as thoughts, "Mom, please don't be sad. I'm with Jacob and he will take care of me, and most of all, Mom, I'm happy. Just remember I will always love you. I will always be near and all you need do to talk is to call out to me. I will be there."

Then Tyler watched as Sara moved over to stand next to her father, Jack, "Daddy, please don't be sad. I am very happy. Jacob will watch out for me. He will take care of me. I love you and always will." Jack looked forward toward the two graves and whispered, "Love you too, Kitten."

Seeing the two spirits together Dr. Schiller's arm once again went around Tyler's shoulder and he squeezed again, a knowing smile on his face.

Tyler nodded his head at Sara and then returned her smile.

Tyler could see, in Sara's eyes, a sparkle he knew too well.

He was about to cry and then he heard her say softly, more a thought than actual utterances, "Thank you, Tyler, for helping. Now, we are both together and home,"

Looking on, Dr. Schiller smiled. Operation "Yankee Boy" was complete.

Made in the USA
Charleston, SC
03 August 2014